CRAIG SPENCE-
SHERIFF

A HUMANE METHOD OF ENFORCEMENT

CRAIG SPENCE-
SHERIFF
A HUMANE METHOD OF ENFORCEMENT

JR CONWAY

CITIOFBOOKS, INC.
3736 Eubank NE Suite A1
Albuquerque, NM 871113579
www.citiofbooks.com
Hotline: 1 (877) 3892759
Fax: 1 (505) 9307244

Ordering Information:

Quantity sales. Special discounts are available on quantity purchases by corporations, associations, and others. For details, contact the publisher at the address above.

Printed in the United States of America.

ISBN13:   Softcover   979-8-89391-101-5
               eBook   979-8-89391-102-2

Library of Congress Control Number: 2024909118

Table of Contents

CHAPTER 1

EVERYONE WAS IN an unusual jovial mood as they gathered for the morning meeting. Fred Driskell from CPI had been invited by Steve Lolly to today's meeting and there was a lot of back slapping between him, Steve and Kevin. Though it was passed time for the meeting to start, Craig sat and watched, reluctant to disrupt what he was observing. *These guys have worked together and successfully closed several complicated cases, they deserve to be in high spirits,* Craig thought. He stood up and began to clap his hands. The room became quiet, and everybody's attention was on him. He Spoke.

"It's not often that I see my staff in such high spirits. It could be that you deserve to be. I've taken the time to review the department's performance recently. We've never done it before, but I think it might be good to check back and see what we learned from operational decisions we made and previous cases we've worked. Sherrie, you want to go first. What operational decisions did we make recently that impacted the department either negatively or positively?"

"Sheriff," Sherrie began. "Steve, Kevin and I just finished our first draft of our proposed budgets for next year. The impact of the decision to hire CPI, on the jail's budget, is fresh in my mind. Last year we budgeted two hundred twenty thousand dollars and some change to pay salaries for deputies used as guards at the hospital and County Courts. We spent a little over two hundred thirty thousand. Quite a bit over budget. This year the commissioners approved only one hundred ninety-eight thousand dollars for these types of services and by using CPI's people we'll spend less than one hundred seventy thousand. The savings comes from lower hourly cost and having to pay no overtime. A second benefit was the availability of personnel.

One phone call and CPI management saw to it that our needs were met. We learned that a relationship with the right organization, can enhance and augment the capabilities of our department."

Craig leaned back in his chair, placed his hand on his chin with a finger alongside his nose. When he spoke, there was concern in his voice. "Having Fred and Amy's outfit to help us has really worked out well for the county, but we can't continue to rely on CPI without a plan B." Craig paused for a long moment then continued. "It was inevitable that other outfits would try and move into the area. CPI is beginning to get some competition. I understand they have been out bid on several of their oil field contracts and could lose Sweetwater Coal."

"What does that have to do with us," Kevin inquired.

"I'm not much on business strategies," Craig began. "but out on the ranch, when the grass in an area became scarce, my dad would move the cattle to an area where the grass was more plentiful. CPI has some large contracts in Montana, South Dakota and Colorado. If they keep getting under bid, they may move their operations, anyway we need to give it some thought. What say you Fred?"

"The competition in our business has picked up," Fred said. "But that's not my greatest concern. The 24/7 operation of the business is beginning to take its toll on Amy's health, and I've got some serious business decisions to make. I don't expect any drastic changes in the immediate future. We've still got contracts that will carry us through the end of next year."

Turning to Steve, Craig continued. "Looking back, what did we do that helped the department?"

"Boss, I think we all agree that bringing CPI on board was probably the best move that had the greatest impact on this department's performance, but I also believe that our all-out support of the state and helping them bust up that auto theft operation has done wonders for this department's image and how it's thought of in law enforcement circles."

"Ok Kevin, what impressed you about the department's performance in recent months?"

"I'm a little biased sheriff," Kevin began. "I think the way we handled the brass bushing situation really put the department in good stead with the corporate community. The word is out among the CEO's and managers at the trona mines, the other coal mines and oil companies about the way we solved the case of the missing bushing and how you handled the situation to save a man's career and save a company major embarrassment at the same time."

"Sheriff," Sherrie spoke up. "Even though we're generally able to keep stuff out of the media circles, it's almost impossible to control word of mouth. You may not know it, but you're a hero in much of Sweetwater County. Your handling of Sister Patricia Anne, Kenneth Boutros and Tom Hastert has gotten around to the coffee clutches, the ladies clubs, the bars and civic associations. The decisions you made in each of those instances reflects favorably on the department. If you're planning on running for another term- I hope- you've got a pretty good shot."

"There'll be a bit of thinking about that over the coming days," Craig responded. "In the meantime, we have another situation that we need to sink our teeth into." Craig took his note book out of his shirt pocket and directed his remarks to Kevin. "This weekend I called you and canceled the raid in Rock Springs. That was because Chief Kessler notified me that he had identified a person in his department that was informing the suspects of police plans. Also, our man on surveillance in the place reported that no activity was going on in any of the rooms. I'm going to meet with him and Chief Kessler at noon. I'll get back to you as soon as I know something. Sherrie, what cha got?"

"You remember the teenager that was molested by her father and who tried to commit suicide? She was released to her mother this morning. Her father is still being held here in lieu of a two hundred fifty-thousand-dollar bond. The truck driver with the infected shingles is still in lockup. We'll be moving him to a regular patient's room later today. We transferred one of our inmates, Paul Schroder, to lock up at the hospital. We're holding him on a warrant out of Mesa, AR. He was complaining about having a pain in his side. That's all I have Sheriff."

"How did we get ahold of Schroder?" Craig inquired.

"Just luck," Sherrie replied. "One of our patrolmen saw him begging for money over at the mall and just thought he'd check him out. According to the deputies' report Schroder told him that he had been robbed and needed to get some money for a bus ticket to Salt Lake. When the deputy ran the name that Schroder gave him through NCIC, he got a hit out of Arizona. They want him for knifing a guy on a construction site."

"Is this gonna be one of those cases where we hold him, feed him, take care of his medical needs and then they decide they don't want him?" Craig asked.

"Don't think so," Sherrie replied. "They've got him on an attempted murder charge."

"Anything Steve?" Craig inquired.

"Yeah boss," Steve started. "I've got an update on the situation at the Silver Dollar. Our guy over there asked me to check out records at the county because he had heard one of the maintenance people say that he was going to block off the parking lot so that there would be room for a truck to take the Silver Dollar Sign down. I stopped by the county clerk's office on the way to work this morning and there's been a complete change of ownership and name changes. The new owners are out of Pocatello, Idaho. The restaurant has been split from the rest of the operation and will be called the "Wagon Wheel." The Bar and dance hall will be called the "Silver Spur." They've also pulled a permit to do some remodeling."

"That's going to change things for us." Craig said. "Let's pull our guy and when I meet with chief Kessler today, we'll come up with a plan. Kevin, I want you at that meeting. You got anything going that will keep you from being there?"

"No Sir," Kevin responded. "I'll be there."

Maggie was already at her desk when Matt Kessler got to police headquarters. There was not the usual jovial *"Morning Maggi"* or *"Hi Maggie, anything happen I need to know about."* It was as though she wasn't even there. In fact, she got a chill the atmosphere was so cold. Matt hadn't been in his office but a short time when the intercom lit up. "Maggie, come in here," he said.

She stood up, took a couple deep breaths, grabbed her pad and with a straight back and head held high entered Matts office. He was holding the phone receiver to his ear, apparently waiting for someone to come on. Then she heard him say, "OK Craig I'll see you about noon." He hung up the phone.

"Yes sir," she said as professionally as she could, "You wanted to see me"

Matt recognized the stiffness in her manner and didn't respond. Instead he opened the center drawer of his desk and took out a large pad. He fumbled with some pens that were in a cup on his desk as if he was looking for a particular pen, then he spoke.

"I don't seem to have a pencil may I borrow yours?"

"I only have the one---" she started but Matt cut her off. "you won't need it," he said.

That didn't quiet the pounding that she felt in her chest. She was sitting with her legs crossed and her steno pad resting on her knee, pencil in her right hand at the ready. She placed the pencil in Matts outstretched hand. After he made some entries on his pad, he swiveled his chair so that he was facing her.

"You know I've never met your husband," he began. "What's his name?

"His name is Ernest," Maggie responded.

"You told me that Ernest lost a lot of money at the Silver Dollar. What else has he told you about the gambling goings on over there?" "Ernest and I have had no conversations about the silver dollars operations. We came very close to divorce over his money losses. The only thing that prevented it was my fear of what would happen if I

were alone."

"Looking at the situation the two of you are in, I'd say he's in no position to be much of a protector," Matt said without looking up from his pad. "What type of work does he do?"

"He's the district manager for a large construction company, "Maggie replied. "He's six feet three and two hundred seventy pounds. I know it's a false sense of security, but I feel safer with him in the house. A bunch of them beat him up a while back, and I think they would have eventually had him killed, but if they did, they would no longer have anything over my head and this source of information would go away."

"Does Ernest know that we know that you have been an informant for the Silver Dollar people?" There was some concern in Matts voice.

"You told me not to say anything to anybody," Maggie was beginning to tear up and her voice was high pitched. "I feel so bad about this whole mess."

"The thing that hurts me most about this mess is that you betrayed my trust and didn't have enough faith in me to bring your problem to me. I don't feel that I can trust you with the inner workings of this department anymore. I'm not going to fire you because I don't want to jeopardize your wellbeing. I am going to move you to another job and location. Clean out your desk and move to the receptionist section at the front of the building. I'll work out your schedule later this afternoon."

"Thank you for not firing me Matt," the sobs had begun again as Maggie followed Matt to the office door. "What reason do I give to the reception staff for the move?"

"Tell them you can no longer work the hours required as my secretary. I'll make the official announcement this afternoon."

Jeff Flores, the person the sheriff's office had hanging out at the Silver Dollar, was the first to arrive for the one o'clock meeting. Jeff appeared to be your typical ranch hand type; a well beaten cowboy hat, a bushy mustache and unshaven face; a wool shirt covered by a leather vest, jeans and a well-worn pair of cowboy boots. He had bowlegs, like most genuine cowboys, and he had a slow gait to his walk. His looks were deceiving.

Jeff had been a highway patrolman in the state of Indiana. He was a member of the state's mounted patrol, the highway patrol's championship pistol team and had won several fast draw competitions. He also had a black belt in martial arts. During a fourth of July parade a dog ran out into the street and spooked his horse. The horse reared, and his hind feet slipped on the asphalt causing it to fall. The animal came down on Jeff crushing his rib cage and severely injuring his back. After several months of hospitalization and rehab Jeff enrolled in a martial arts course to regain his strength and mobility. Though he felt fit to go back to work he was offered a medical retirement and he took it.

While getting a hair cut in the local barber shop, Jeff picked up a cattleman's magazine and saw an advertisement by the Wyoming Cattleman's Association for a range rider whose job would be to deter and investigate cattle rustling. He applied, was interviewed and because of his law enforcement experience, his familiarity with horses and knowledge of firearms, got the job. Over the years he had become good friends with Craig and Fred Driskell. He was on Fred's payroll as a part time security officer and periodically protected crime scenes or did surveillance for both.

There was no one at the front desk so Jeff called out. "Anybody home?" Matt came out of his office.

"I'm the Chief of police here, can I help you?" Matt spoke sternly.

"I'm Jeff Flores," Jeff said, sticking his hand out to shake Matts. "Craig Spence told me to meet him here for a meeting." Matt took Jeff's hand and lead him into his office.

"Craig's not here yet but should be shortly," Matt said. What do you do for Craig?"

"Generally, whatever he asks," Jeff replied. "I've been hanging out at the Dollar."

"Ah Ha!" Matt exclaimed. "Craig told me he had somebody over there. Well, take a seat." Matt motioned to a chair in front of his desk. "Coffee, water or anything?" Jeff Declined.

It was only a few moments more that Craig came in with Kevin in tow. Matt directed them to chairs that he had positioned around a small conference table that he generally used for meetings with his staff. He took the chair at the head of the table and began the meeting.

"I want to thank you Craig for coming over and bringing your guys. I'm really at a loss as to the operations over at the Silver Dollar. In case your people are not aware, every time we planned a move on them over there, they were way ahead of us. We even put an informant over there, not knowing that your man Jeff here, was also in there. Just by luck we found out that they had an informant right here in my shop. I figure we need to work closer together if we're going to take these guys down."

"Do we need to know who the leaker was Matt?" Craig asked. "I haven't even told my people that I know who the informant

was. I want to keep it to myself because I don't want the people at the Dollar to know that we know," Matt replied. "Not that I don't trust you guys but the fewer of us that know the easier it is to keep it secret and I can use the informant to our advantage."

"Gotcha," Craig indicated that he understood. "Well we may be in luck. I found out today that the place has been sold and a permit has been pulled to do some remodeling. The name has been changed.

The restaurant will be the Wagon Wheel and the bar will be the Silver Spur. Everything will be shut down until the construction work is finished."

"Hell, that being the case I guess this meeting is premature," Matt said.

"Hold on," Jeff spoke up. "you guys may have just been handed the goose that laid the golden egg. I've been hanging around that place for almost six months and I haven't been able to figure out where the gambling operation goes on. I know it's happening, and I know the people who gamble there, but where- I'm stumped. I'd bet my horses feed bag that this tiger is not going to change its stripes. After the place reopens, they'll be doing just what they've done before."

"If you're through talking in riddles Jeff, maybe you'll tell us what you're getten at," Kevin chimed in on the conversation.

"Yeh Jeff, you got something to say spit it out," Craig urged. "They haven't started construction yet," Jeff began. "Get someone or maybe even a couple of people on the construction crew. You'll be able to get a firsthand lay of the land over there."

"I think we can be assured that the new owners are going to use a construction firm that they know, trust and have used many times before," Craig said almost as if he was thinking out loud. "If they use subcontractors for such things as electrical, plumbing, and wallboard, your idea may give us an inside look. I don't have anyone on my staff that has any construction in their background. How about you Matt?" he asked.

"Not that I'm aware of and I wouldn't be able to spare a man from the force if I did," was Matts reply.

The four men sat for more than an hour discussing alternative approaches to gaining information and developing investigative strategies. It was decided that Kevin would be the one to keep an eye out for any activity regarding preparations to start construction; the posting of advertisements for construction specialties or laborers; the positioning of equipment and such. Since Jeff Flores was a frequenter of the local bars, he volunteered to keep an eye out for newcomers to town. Both Matt and Craig would try and come up with people who had construction experience that would be able to be recruited as special deputies or informants.

Matt left the meeting and as promised went to the reception area to announce Maggie's addition to the staff. The area was rather undescriptive; A desk in the center of the room where the supervisor of the section sat; two desks on opposite sides of the room; several filing cabinets along one wall; two stations at a counter where staff members provided available services to the public (general information, copies of police and accident reports, applicable forms and brochures). They looked out into the waiting area through a glass partition that served as protection from potentially dangerous instances.

Matt gathered the staff, including Maggie, around the supervisor's desk and explained to them that Maggie would be joining the team and while she would assist with normal operations of the section, she would also address matters pertaining to department operations, citizen complaints and accept service from the courts on behalf of the department. No one had any questions, so Matt walked from the room never once looking in Maggie's direction.

CHAPTER 2

IT WAS A slow day at the Department, so Craig was able to get home on time for dinner. When he walked through the door, he could smell sweet potatoes. He could smell meat too, but he couldn't figure out what It was.

"It Sure smells good in here," he called out as he walked into the kitchen.

"I Iey you?" Martha answered as she walked toward him whipping her hands on a towel. "Nice to have you home early," she said as they gave each other a peck on the lips. She then pulled out a chair from the table and motioned for him to sit.

"What's that meat I smell," Craig asked.

"Baked Pork Chops," a voice came from a small pantry of to the side of the kitchen. "How's my Daddy," Katie asked lovingly as she came up carrying a saucepan filed with peas and gave him a kiss on a spot thinning on top of his head.

"How goes it Kitten," Craig responded. "You been making your Mom behave?"

"I've been meaning to speak to you about that?" Kattie replied with a chuckle.

"Don't you be telling tales out of school," Martha spoke up. "Something I should Know?" Asked Craig.

"NO!!" Exclaimed Martha. Katie walked over and put an arm around Martha's shoulders.

"Mom," she said. "I told you I was going to tell Dad. I just forgot yesterday.

Dad, For the past couple of days, your wife has been cleaning out the closets and boxes stored in the extra bedroom upstairs. Today, she made me take tons of stuff in bags down to the Goodwill."

"Tattle Tale," Martha said as she took Katie's arm off her shoulder.

"Think you're over doing it a little Doll." Craig inquired.

"It wasn't easy, "Martha responded. "I'd do a little and rest a little. I've got to move around and do things. Being tired is a way of life right now but I'm not going to become a veg." There was a sternness in her voice that Craig hadn't heard for a long time.

"Let's eat," Katie said as she put a platter of Porkchops on the table.

After a great dinner, Craig settled into his favorite chair with the newspaper, and was listening to the local news on the TV when the phone rang. He saw that Katie was getting it, so his attention stayed with what was on the news.

"It's for you Dad," Katie called out. Grudgingly Craig moved across the room where a phone sat on a small stand.

"Spence here," he said. "what!! How did that happen?" There was a slight pause before he spoke again. "What's being done?" Another pause, a little longer this time. "Okay have somebody pick me up."

"What's going on," Martha asked with concern in her voice.

"A prisoner that we were holding at the hospital has escaped," Craig replied. "We've never had anyone get out of lockup…"

The doctor didn't get around to seeing Paul Schroder until late in the afternoon. All day while he was waiting, he was trying to figure a way to get out. He had thought that he might jump the guard when he brought his dinner. *The guard was rather elderly, maybe in his late 50's.*

He could take him easily he thought, but then he'd have to go through the hospital to get out and he didn't remember how to get out. He discarded that idea. Then he noticed something. The windows, he had installed many of that kind. They were held in place by two large flat head screws that went into the window frame. If the screws were removed a push would make the window swivel open. The problem would be to get the screws out. They made sure he had nothing on him when they locked him up.

While he was running ideas through his mind, they came in with an ultrasound machine and used it to assess what was causing the pain in his side. Not long after they had left, the doctor came in and told him that he was full of gas, "you're bloated" he had said, and he would give him something to make him fart. Shortly after the doctor left the guard let a nurse in and she gave him 2 capsules and a cup of water.

The guard came in with his dinner. The food was on a hard paper tray and there was a package of plastic utensils. There was a plastic spoon, fork and knife. Paul realized that he was in fact hungry and there was a chicken leg, a thigh and a wing for meat, and mashed potatoes and gravy along with green beans. There even was a napkin. He didn't have to use toilet paper like in jail. While he was eating, he had another idea.

The guard eventually came in to pick up the tray. Paul had spread his napkin over the top of all the bones and other scraps left on it. The guard, having done this work for some time, picked up the napkin.

"Okay Paul. Where's the knife?" The guard asked.

"Didn't I put it on the tray," Paul asked trying to sound surprised. "Give me the knife or I'll take your bed out and strip you down

to your skin," said the guard.

Paul reached under his pillow and pulled out the plastic knife. He placed it on the tray and the guard left the room. *That didn't turn out too well, he thought.* He looked all around the room. It had been converted from a regular patient room so all the fixtures, oxygen connections and switches had been removed and plates put over the openings. On the

"How long do we figure he's been gone?" Steve asked.

"The guard turned the lights out at 8:00 pm and he was on the bed," Fred said. "He checked him again at 8:45pm and he noticed the window open, so he has at most a forty- five- minute lead on us. He's bare foot and wearing a hospital gown. I don't think he's very far."

Kevin stuck his head out of the window and called to the group to come closer. He was shining his flashlight at the palm of his hand. When Craig, Steve, Fred and Amy were directly under the window, he spoke.

"I guess we're gonna have to start giving these guys a manicure before we lock them up." He held the palm of his hand out where everyone could see what he had. "I found these little pieces of fingernail on the floor under where the plate had come off the wall. I figure he made a screwdriver out of a finger nail and managed to get the screw out of the plate; then he used the plate to unlock the screws in the window frame and he's out of here."

"As many times as, I've adjusted the shades in those windows, I've never noticed those screw locks," Fred said.

"They were painted over and looked like the frame. Unless you were looking for em and knew where they were you wouldn't see em," Kevin said. Fred's radio began to squeal.

"CPI One here," Fred said into the radio. A big smile came across his face and he said, "Great job." Then he continued. "Put him in the back of the patrol vehicle and bring him back to the hospital." He then turned to Craig, "They got him."

"Steve," Craig called out. "I want you to get with Hospital Security and have them get their maintenance people to take a drill and round out the heads of all the screws in those plates on the wall. This guy has shown us a weakness in our system so let's make sure and make it harder to get out by eliminating it."

While Craig was speaking the CPI patrol truck pulled up. Paul was in the bed of the truck, on his back, each arm and leg handcuffed to one of the tie-down rings in the trucks bed. He could be heard yelling at a sheriff's deputy that was standing on the trucks rear bumper as the truck pulled to a stop near the group of lawmen.

"The least you guys could do is try and miss some of the rough spots. You're killing my back." Craig moved over to the truck and leaned over the side. While he checked the cuffs to make sure they weren't too tight he was speaking to Paul.

"Not very comfy, huh?" Just think, you had a nice warm, comfortable bed and you decided to leave it. I'm not sympathetic. What did you get into? you stink." The hospital gown Paul was wearing was filthy. The Deputy that was riding the bumper spoke up. "One of the families living where we found him raises rabbits.

He was curled up in one of the hutches."

"Get him cleaned up, would ya Fred," Craig asked. "After you do, put him in the jump suit he wore up here. I'll go in and get the paperwork done. I'm taking him back to jail.

CHAPTER 3

EVEN THOUGH IT had been a long night, Craig was up early and was having his usual morning cup of coffee when Martha came in with the day's newspaper and sat it on the table beside him.

"Thanks doll, it hadn't come when I checked earlier," Craig advised as he got up to get her a cup of coffee.

"I smelled the coffee and as I was coming by, I heard the "plop" as it hit the door," Martha said through a yawn. "I was asleep before you came in last night, how'd it go?"

Craig spent the next few moments relating how the detainee had escaped and where he had been found. Martha listened with interest and chuckled about the escapee being found in the rabbit hutch.

"What do you plan to do with him?" Martha waited while Craig sipped his coffee, then he answered.

"Soon's I get to the office I'm calling Mesa and tell them to stop procrastinating and come get him. I could hold him and charge him with escaping, but I don't want him."

"Why don't you just load him up and take him down there? She asked. "It's not that far."

"I'll give that some thought. Might be able to get CPI to do it. We'll see," Craig responded as he opened the paper to the business section and took another sip of his coffee. There in the middle of the page, a posting caught his eye. It read, ***"Casino Conglomerate purchases local Restaurant and Bar."***

"Well I guess it's official. The Silver Dollar has been sold," he said to Martha.

"Oh? Who bought it?" she inquired.

"I'll read what's here," Craig said. "The headline says, Casino **Conglomerate purchases local Restaurant and Bar.** The article says, *according to the Sweetwater County Clerk's Office, the Silver Dollar in Rock Springs has been purchased by the South West Entertainment Corporation, headquartered in Pocatello, Idaho. It is expected that after some renovations to the existing property, the grand opening should occur in about forty-five days, said Tony Castillo, who will be the General Manager. The name of the new lounge will be The Silver Spur and the restaurant portion of the operation will be called The Wagon Wheel. The Silver Spur will be closed on Sunday, Monday and Tuesday but will be open Wednesday, Thursday, Friday and Saturday. Professional entertainment will be featured on Friday and Saturday. The restaurant will be open every day, Castillo said."* Craig folded the paper and took another sip of his coffee.

"Wasn't the chief over at the Springs having trouble with the Silver Dollar?" Martha asked.

"Yeh," Craig answered. "I think this purchase might solve some of his woes but then again, it could be the beginning of a whole new batch – Well gotta go Doll. See you this evening," and with a peck on her forehead he was headed for the door.

As usual, Craig's operating staff gathered for the morning meeting where they briefed one another of what had occurred the previous day and night; discussed current operational investigations and strategized about methods and procedures by which to proceed. Today Craig started the meeting with a presentation regarding the Southwest Entertainment Corp.

"In This morning's paper, he began- was an article pertaining to the sale of the Silver Dollar. It confirms that the place has been sold to an entertainment outfit out of Idaho. It also indicates who the general Manager will be and what the new names associated with the business are going to be. Anyone heard of this outfit before?" No was unanimous among the staff.

"How about a guy named Toney Costello?" Craig asked. Again, there was a unanimous no and then Steve recanted.

"Just a minute," Steve said. "Kevin, what was that guy's name you ran across sleeping in his car down by the river several years back? Remember when you checked him out there was a BOLO (Be on the lookout) on him and he got upset when you called him Mr. Costello instead of Cos-ty-o. The two L's are pronounced Y and actually sounds like Cos-ste-o."

"I remember bringing a guy in on a warrant or something about four or five years ago. I'd have to go back through my notebooks to see. I've got them dated by year, and the events by name. After the meeting I could look."

"Why don't you do that," Craig suggested. "I've just got a feeling we may want to get out ahead of, I don't know what, but I've got a feelin. Oh- and while you're at it, call Bannock County in Idaho and find out all you can about this entertainment corporation."

Craig pulled a folded newspaper from his inside jacket pocket and passed it to Kevin. He then started the rotation of staff members giving their reports starting with Sherrie Mullens.

What's going on Sherrie?" He asked.

"We got Paul put away last night so that he won't pull another disappearing act. We also put a call in to the Sheriff of Maricopa County where Mesa is located and asked what their plans were for returning him to their custody."

"Beginning to think you've been here too long Sherrie," Craig stated.

"I beg your pardon Sheriff. Sherrie had shock in her voice. "You're beginning to read my mind and that's scary," Craig said through a chuckle and there could be an audible sigh from Sherrie. "What did you find out," Craig asked.

"They are preparing for some big convention and they need all their spare deputies for traffic control. It will be another week before they'll be able to break someone loose to come up here."

"Get ahold of them and offer to deliver if they'll foot the bill." Craig instructed. "What else you got?"

"We have another detainee at the hospital," Sherrie said. "A female that was put in a little after 10 PM last night. Apparently, she was pounding on the door at a residence on Bridger Avenue, claiming that it was her house and demanding that the people get out."

"Any idea who she is or where she came from?" Craig asked. "She had no ID on her, no wallet or purse," Sherrie answered.

"According to the police officer's report, she was driven over to the bus station to see if the employees there could recognize her, with no luck. She had not come in on any of yesterday's buses. They took her picture at the hospital and are checking the truck stops to see if anyone will recognize her. Amy from CPI is having her people clean her up, I guess she was smelly. That's all I have Sheriff."

"OK," Craig said. What you got Steve?"

"The deputy that I generally have over at the Department of Motor Vehicles has called in sick, so I'll be spending most of the day over there verifying Vin Numbers, boss."

"And you Kevin," Craig continued to inquire.

"I'll just be running down the info on the entertainment company Sheriff, Kevin responded.

"Alright," Craig said as he pushed his chair back from the table. "Let's hope we have a productive day. Let's get at it…"

Just as Amy was getting ready for bed, the phone rang, and she answered it. Fred could hear her side of the conversation. "Male or female," he heard her say. "OK, I'll be right there," he heard her say before hanging up the phone.

"Want me to take it, babe," he offered.

"No, it's a female," She said. "I'll see what we've got and call one of our female guards in to take over."

When she arrived, she was met by the hospital security guard who briefed her regarding the situation. He advised her that the female in lockup was incoherent and un-communitive. He told her that when the female was brought in, she was very combative and had to be placed in restraints. She had been given a sedative by the ER doctor and was now sitting on the floor. He advised Amy that there was a mattress in the room, but no bed and she was dressed in a hospital gown.

When Amy reached lock up, she looked into the room through the observation port in the door. She could see no one. She could see the mattress and the hospital gown was on it. Across the room, the shades on the windows were closed and she could see the female's reflection, stark naked, sitting on the floor, against the door right below the observation port.

As she watched, Amy noticed that the individual appeared to be fairly attractive with shoulder length stringy brown hair, estimated that she weighed about 110 pounds, and maybe, if standing would be about five foot-eight or nine inches tall. As she watched she noticed that the person was masturbating. She decided to just let her be and went to the phone to call in a guard that would be capable of handling the situation.

After waiting for approximately forty-five minutes, Amy heard someone talking and laughing with the hospital staff at the nurse's station up the hall. It was Tess Hawkins, a retired nurse who worked part time for CPI, generally at the hospital where she was highly respected and was great at dealing with the unexpected. Amy thought of Tess as being roly-poly. Her legs were short and stubby, and her hips were very large, out of proportion with her upper body. She always wore a smile on her face which was surrounded by well- groomed steel gray hair.

"What we got boss?" She asked Amy as she waddled down the hall toward her.

"Brace yourself," Amy replied.

They both moved to the door to lockup and peered through the port. The person was now sitting on the floor in the middle of the room. In her left hand she was holding a brown glob and with the fingers of her right hand she was peeling some off and putting it in her mouth.

"OH SHIT!!! Tess exclaimed. "That's what it is," Amy agreed.

"Amy," Tess said in a calm voice. "I'm going to the nurse's station and get a couple of hospital gowns in case she decides to use us for target practice. If you will get a couple of hands full of paper towels from the bathroom, we'll see if we can separate her from it without getting smeared." She was off to the nurse's station.

It turned out not to be as terrifying a task as was anticipated. When Tess and Amy entered the room, their uniforms covered with hospital gowns-all but their backs- the woman just stared up at them, hands outstretched as if she was trying to show them what she had. Amy gave Tess several paper towels and they proceeded to remove the smelly excrement from her hands. She just watched them without any comment or effort to prevent them from removing the stuff. Apparently, whatever the ER doctor gave her had rendered her very dossal. Getting her into the shower and cleaning her up was without incident.

When the woman was returned to the lockup room there were two Rock Springs police officers waiting at the security area. Amy stopped to converse with them while Tess put the woman away.

"Hi Guys." Amy greeted the one closest to her. "If you came to help us clean this lady up, you're too late." Both officers laughed aloud.

"I'm officer Cranston," the one closest to Amy said. "We were following up on the lady you have in detention and at the truck stop west of town the employees had found this purse in the ladies rest room." He handed Amy a small red purse and continued. "In the purse is a driver's license with a picture that very much matches the one we took of her when we picked her up." Amy opened the purse and looked at the license which was inserted in a plastic covered slot.

"Yep," she said. "That's her. The name on the license is Judy Stevenson and it was issued by the State of Utah and her address is in the city of Sandy. She's sedated right now but if you'll leave it with me when she's alert, I'll verify that the purse is hers."

Amy was still looking in the purses compartments when she found another interesting slip of paper. It was the receipt from a Greyhound bus ticket from Provo, Utah to Evanston, Wyoming. Without looking up she said, "It's going to be interesting to hear how she got way up here…"

Judy Stevenson's life was never a bed of roses. She was born out of wedlock and raised by a single mother who suffered from Schizophrenia. Early on she began to show signs of mental illness. Eventually she exhibited such bazaar behavior that she was committed to treatment facilities. Over most of her teenage years she was in and out of different health centers, both private and state to diagnose her problem and provide effective treatment.

Judy, now twenty-Four years old, had been admitted to a facility located in Provo, Utah. After some months with no recognizable success, arrangements were made with the State hospital in Evanston, Wyoming, where a renowned mental health professional was conducting Studies. She was given a plastic vial containing two little white pills and told to take them if she became anxious or apprehensive. She was put on a bus and told that she would be met by representatives from the Wyoming State Hospital upon arrival in Evanston. They would be waiting in the bus terminal and holding a sign with her name on it, she would then present them with a letter which would introduce her and provide information as to why she was there.

wall beside his bed had been an electric outlet. The plate over it was held in place by a screw with a concaved head. It would be impossible to get anything other than a small screwdriver in there to turn it.

He was picking the chicken out of his teeth with his fingernail when he got a great idea. He hadn't cut his fingernails for a while and they were nice and long. The thumb nails were the strongest. He began gnawing at the sides of his right thumb nail until he had formed a nice flat blade in the center. He laid on his bed until the guard turned out the lights in the room, then with his left hand he felt were the screw went into the plate. He had to gnaw on the right nail several more times to get it small enough to fit the slot in the screw. Very slowly he applied pressure until the screw started to loosen. When the plate was off, he crawled over to the window and placed the edge into the head of a locking screw. He could get just enough of the edge of the plate into the grove so that it wouldn't slip. The screw began to turn. After a few turns the edge of the plate bent. *Use the other edge,* he told himself. He turned the plate over and did the same to the second anchor screw. When it came out, he pushed one side of the window and it rotated. He leaned out and realized that it was only a short distance to the ground…

Sheriff Craig Spence along with Steve Lolly, met Fred and Amy Driskell at the hospital. Fred and Amy were standing outside the window that their detainee had escaped through.

"Hi ya, you two," Craig said in greeting.

"Hello Sheriff," Fred responded. "Sorry you had to come out for this."

"There was nothing worth reading in the paper anyway," Craig said with a chuckle. "What's going on?"

"Kevin is crawling along the floor in there trying to figure out how Paul got the plate he used off the wall," Amy said. "We've got officers on foot out in the field between here and the highway, we have a patrolman and other men on foot in the residential area south of us. I believe a couple of your patrolmen are out on the highway."

When the bus pulled off the interstate to enter the town of Evanston, Judy began to experience anxiety. She began to be apprehensive about what was probably in store for her at the place where she was headed. Judy took out the vial with the pills in it and as she took off the top, she remembered that the last pills she had been given made her feel weird and she couldn't think straight. She took the pills and dumped them in a pocket behind the seat in front of her. When she exited the bus at the terminal, she did not go inside.

She crossed the street and walked away. She walked until she came upon a truck stop. Young and attractive, she had little difficulty in soliciting a ride from a trucker. When the trucker pulled out onto I-80 he headed east. He told Judy that he was headed to Mississippi and she indicated that she would go wherever he was going. As they proceeded up the highway and engaged in casual conversation, the trucker became aware that something was not right with Judy. She began to ramble and kept wandering off whatever topic they were discussing. The situation was not good and when he came upon the turnoff for Rock Springs, he took it and pulled into a Texaco truck stop. He told her that he had to use the bathroom and suggested that she go too because it would be a long time before they'd stop again. When Judy came back to the parking lot the truck was gone. The realization that she had been dumped made her furious and her anger caused her body to shake violently and she sat down on the ground until she got control of herself, but she was confused, she had no idea where she was, but in the distance she could see a building that looked like the building she lived in-in Sandy, Utah. She got up and began walking toward it…

Dr. Fenster, a cardiologist, was on staff to care for individuals in detention this week and she met with Tess, the CPI Security Guard at nine AM the morning after the feces episode. Tess handed the Dr. her report which outlined everything that happened related to the detainee from the time she took over the post until the present. "Has there been any further incidence of pop eating sense the one you report here? Dr. Fenster asked Tess.

"No doctor, Tess responded. "She actually slept most all night except to go pee once."

"Do we know where she came from prior to being picked up here?" Fenster was trying to establish a starting point for her eventual inquiry.

"The only thing we have is this purse that she left at the truck stop west of town." Tess began." Papers inside indicate that she may be from Sandy, Utah and the receipt of a bus ticket shows that she may have ridden a bus to Evanston. There is no indication of how she got here other than the purse being at the truck stop makes me believe she caught a ride."

"Have you looked all through the purse?" Dr. Fenster asked. "No," Tess replied. "Once we identified her, we stopped looking through it."

"May I have it," the doctor asked. Tess passed her the purse and watched as she began to systematically poke around into each compartment and pouch.

"Aha!" The doctor exclaimed as she stood looking at a business card. "Dr. Elmo Thurston, LDS Psychiatrics- Provo, Utah." She read. "And there is a phone number. I'm going up to the nurse's station and call. I'll be back." While she waited Tess began putting the contents of the purse back. She tried to put everything in some semblance of order, as if it was hers. Then she waited.

Almost an hour had passed before Tess saw Dr. Fenster coming down the hall toward her. She had a pad in her hand and a yellow pencil in her mouth. She was fishing in the pocket of her white coat for something. Just as she got to Tess, she pulled out the business card that she had found in the purse. She took the pencil out of her mouth and began to talk to Tess.

"Here," she said as she handed Tess the card. "You might need this information for your report. Sorry it took so long but I kept getting answering machines. It took forever to get a human on the line, When I told the lady that answered why I was calling, she went and got Dr. Thurston and brought him to the phone." She made some notes on the pad she was carrying and continued to speak. "Your ward in there is supposed to be at the State Hospital in Evanston. Let's give it a go and see if we can talk to her."

Tess led the way and made sure that Judy was away from the door. She was sitting on her mattress with her head on her knees. Tess unlocked the door and let Dr. Fenster into the room.

"Hi Judy," Dr Fenster said as she approached the mattress. "My name is Dr. Fenster and I'm here to try and help you." Dr Fenster paused as her eyes met with Judy's and the Dr. sat on the floor, facing this young lady who stared back at her with blank eyes. The Dr tried once more.

"Do you know where you are Judy?" She asked.

"I think I'm in a hospital," Judy responded. "It smells like a hospital." "You're right," the Dr. confirmed. "Do you remember a Dr. Thurston?"

"Yeh." Judy answered turning her mouth as if she had tasted something sour. "He kept touching me."

"What do you mean?" Dr. Fenster was quizzical.

"He acted like he was checking my heart with that plastic thing, but I knew what he was doing." Tess who had been standing behind the Dr. very quietly, now moved over and sat on the mattress beside Judy.

"Did Dr. Thurston ever tell you that you might be sick?" the Dr. asked.

"He didn't have too," Judy said. "I already knew that. He was supposed to figure out what was wrong."

"You were supposed to go to the State Hospital in Evanston. The people that were at the bus stop to meet you couldn't find you, what happened?" The Dr. waited for Judy to answer. She was looking down at her hands like a little girl who was in trouble.

"I think I got scared," Judy finally said.

"Can you tell me what you were scared off? The Dr asked. "I don't know, I was just scared," Judy said quietly.

"I understand that you were eating your poop last night. How long have you been doing that?" The question caught Judy off guard, and she jerked back sharply.

"Who told you that!" Judy exclaimed. "that's so embarrassing." "How long Judy?" The Dr. Pressed.

"Since I was younger," Judy said. "Maybe since I was a teenager. I just get the urge and I do it." Judy was showing signs of becoming agitated.

"OK Judy," the Dr said as she got to her feet. "That's enough for now. We're going to see if we can figure out what's wrong and help you feel better. You will have to work with us though. There is a doctor at the State Hospital that specializes in cases like yours and we will make arrangements to get you down there." She motioned to Tess that she was ready to leave the room.

Once outside the room Dr. Fenster confided to Tess that though she had never had to deal with a case herself, she had heard of cases where people ate their poop.

"Generally, its associated with liking the smell, taste or feel in a sexual way," she said.

"It's called Coprophilia. It has also been observed in individuals with mental illnesses. This is known as Coprophagia. I'll get with the hospital administrator and see about arranging transport for her to the State hospital." Dr Fenster headed up the corridor toward the nurse's station.

A letter arrived from Arizona requesting the Sheriff of Sweetwater County, WY. To transport one Paul Schroder to the custody of the Sheriff of Maricopa County, Arizona and upon receipt of an appropriate invoice the Sheriff of Sweetwater County, Wy would be reimbursed the cost incurred. That was what Craig had been hoping for, so he hurried and made arrangements with CPI to transport Paul to Arizona.

Fred Driskell decided that he would take the trip, so with one of his male officers riding shotgun he loaded Paul into the company's Tornado.

Paul was dressed in an orange jump suit and handcuffed to a transport belt around his waist. His hands were in front with just enough slack in the cuffs to facilitate his ability to relieve himself. Because he was a known runner, he also had leg irons attached to his ankles. He sat in the passenger's seat and the guard riding shot gun sat in the back directly behind him so that he could thwart any attempts by Paul to get unruly. Fred was curious though about Paul's escape from the hospital. During the ride Fred decided to engage Paul in conversation.

"Paul I'm curious about something," Fred said. "I've been working in those lockup rooms at the hospital for several years and was never aware of those locking screws in those windows. How did you know about them?" Paul who was slouching in the seat drew himself up straight and turned toward Fred.

"I've been in construction most of my life," Paul began. "The contractor that I've been working for puts up commercial buildings. A lot of them have the same kind of windows. When they come the casings are just plain aluminum, no paint. We spray paint them to go with the color of the building. We make sure that the slots in the screw heads ain't filled with paint. Whoever did the one's at the hospital painted over the slots and you couldn't see em."

"Do you have family Paul," Fred asked.

"I got a sister, Paul responded. "She's in Seattle. Got a bunch of kids. Think she works in night clubs as a dancer. Haven't seen her in a couple of years."

"How'd you get to Arizona," Fred inquired.

"Was hanging out with this guy when I was between jobs and he had a computer, and he helped me look for work. We answered a bunch of ads and this contractor in Mesa took me on."

"Where were you when you were hanging out between jobs," Fred asked.

"Oregon," Paul replied. "I worked up there for over a year but got laid off."

"The warrant for your arrest says you're wanted for attempted murder," Fred related. "What happened?"

Paul shifted in the seat and turned toward the window. He stared out the window for a time then he spoke softly.

"The guy who I hurt had been a drinking buddy," he began. "Almost every day after work we'd stop by a bar we liked and have a few. One day he tried to fix me up with this girl he knew, and I told him thanks but no. He kept insisting that I meet her, and I kept telling him I wasn't interested. Finally, guess I'd had enough to drink to be brave, I just blurted it out-Stop trying to hook me up with girls, I'm gay dam it!!"

There was a long pause. Fred nor Paul spoke. They had traveled several miles before Paul broke the silence.

"He was a different person after that. He was mean, called me names, refused to work with me on stuff we had to do. He spread the word to the other guys, but they didn't seem to care. One day I was on my knees laying carpet in a closet, he poked me in the ass with a broom handle and I lost it. I had been using a curved knife to trim the carpet. I f***ed him up pretty good."

"Did he die?" Fred asked.

"I don't know, I don't think so since the warrant says attempted murder," Paul replied.

The highway stretched out before them and all was quiet for a considerable amount of time. Fred always liked driving through this stretch because of the rock formations and the high meadows that could be seen from the road. But today there was something gnawing at him as a result of what Paul had related to him. He spoke to Paul in a respectful manner.

"Maybe you can help me understand something," Fred said. "I've never really been able to understand the Gay phenomena. When did you first realize that you were Gay?"

"No one has ever asked me that question," Paul responded. "I guess no one really cared to know." Paul readjusted his position in the seat, sitting up very straight and half turned to face Fred.

"There were four of us kids in the family," he began. "Three boys and a girl. My sister and I were twins. My brothers liked doing what boys are supposed to do, wrestling with each other, playing sports and going fishing and such. Me, I liked playing with dolls and dressing up in my sister's clothes, didn't like getting dirty and hung out with my Mom a lot. My Dad was not happy with me and tried to make me like what my brothers liked to do. When I showed no interest, he'd call me his Little Queer. I didn't know what a queer was, I just knew I was different." Paul paused again and then continued.

"In grade school I really liked hanging out with the girls at recesses, playing dodge ball, skipping rope, hop skip and jump and that sought of stuff. The favorite names boys called me were punk, sissy and girly boy. There was one boy who befriended me however, and I liked him a lot. I liked my brothers too, but this was different. When we left grade school, he went to a different high school than me and I felt lost and alone," again Paul paused, and Fred glanced over at him and noticed a look of forlorn on his face. Paul started again.

"High school was worst. Guys were always making remarks about the way girls looked or bragging about dates they'd had and what they did, I just didn't fit, but I wasn't alone. There was Thurman. He was like me, different and ostracized. We were in the same classes and spent lots of time together. We talked about the way we felt about things and each other. We were sophomore's when the science teacher took the class on a field trip and Thurman and I sat together on the bus. That's the first time we acted out our feelings. We began to feel each other between our legs, and it felt good to have Thurman doing that. A few days later, I don't remember exactly how long it was, but we Locked ourselves in the furnace room at school. That was the first time we kissed each other. That's when I knew for sure why I felt different about girls and why I was attracted to this boy." Again, there was a long silence. Fred had listened intently at what Paul had relayed to him. In his mind he went back over what Paul had said and realized that his contention about Gays had probably been wrong all these years. It may not be a conscious decision by someone to be gay. Curious, he asked Paul.

"What became of Thurman? Did you guys continue your relationship?"

"When we were Juniors," Paul began. "I found a note stuck in the vents of my locker at school. It was from Thurman. It said that he cared for me dearly, but he didn't want to. He wanted to be like everybody else. He didn't want to be queer. The note ended with- Sorry. He didn't come to school the next day, so I went to his house to talk to him. His mom told me that he had committed suicide..."

CHAPTER 4

KEVIN HAD SPENT several hours speaking with officials in Bannock County, Idaho regarding the South West Entertainment Corporation. From the Clerk's office he learned that the business had filed in several cities within the county over a period of five years. In each filing the Principles were different, and they would be the parent of smaller operations, like a casino or a night club.

From the Sheriff's office of Bannock County, Kevin learned that the Corporation was suspected of running illegal gambling operations. They always apply for and receive licenses to have slot machines and electronic card games. "We've also initiated investigations, based on complaints from legal operators," Kevin was told. "The complaints are that the South West Entertainment Corp. is also operating table games such as Blackjack, Poker and Craps. They've done a great job of hiding these operations. According to the Sheriff's Investigative department they've never been able to catch them at it. Every time they realize that the operation is being looked at, they sell the business to an out of state business that they control, remodel the building, open a restaurant or something, buy a business in another city and get a license to operate gambling there. The Bannock County Sheriff's Office is exerting so much pressure that it is believed that operations are being moved to other states."

Feeling that he had a considerable amount of information, Kevin decided to present it at the next staff meeting. When it became his turn, he laid out what he had learned, and a discussion ensued.

"Why is it that it has been so hard to pin these guys down?" Craig asked.

"Apparently the gambling clientele is not made up of locals," Kevin advised. "They come in from other cities or outside the city limits where the operations are located. So really the Sheriff only has the verbal complaints from legitimate operations to go by. No one comes in and signs a complaint." There was a long pause before Craig spoke.

"Well," he said. "It's Matts baby, but we'll have to support him. I don't want to come in on the tail end of some deal and have to play catch up. You stay on this when you can. Keep your ear to the ground."

Craig took out his little notebook and took some notes. As he put it back in his shirt pocket, he addressed Sherrie Mullins.

"What you got today Sherrie?" he asked.

"The locals have been pretty quiet," she started. "We only have two persons being arraigned today. I did make arrangements for a transport to the State Hospital yesterday. A copy of the report is there on your desk. Other than that, it's been slow."

"You caught up in anything Steve?" Craig asked.

"Not really boss," Steve responded. "Since things are fairly slow around here, I'd like to take a day and go fishing if it's okay with you." "That sounds like a decent request," Craig pondered the idea. "Don't think I've been fishing in a year or two. What day were you planning to go?"

"I thought I'd take tomorrow off," Steve replied. "Wanna go?" "Let's do it," Craig said with a big smile.

"Pick you up about five o'clock in the morning?" Steve advised. "Deal," Craig replied.

Flaming Gorge Reservoir is a fisherman's paradise and located just 25 miles south of the town of Green River. The lake was filled with lake trout, rainbow trout, brown trout, kokanee salmon, small mouth bass and Some catfish. The reservoir covered parts of Wyoming and a section of Utah. Steve pulled his boat, a 21-foot blue and white Star Craft, to Buck Board Marina, the most popular access to the reservoir on the Wyoming side.

After launching, Steve headed south on the lake. It was 6:30 am and there was no wind, the water was smooth as glass allowing the boat to glide effortlessly across its surface. After cruising for twenty minutes Steve slowed the boat and brought it to a stop where the shoreline consisted of high, majestic cliffs and the rising sun, shining near their tops, was reflecting off their face, accentuating the orange, red, green and yellow colors in the stone.

Steve let out an anchor to prevent the boats drifting away from the area he wanted to fish. He'd fished here before and it was very productive. Craig set up a lawn chair he'd brought along and set up to fish off the boat's stern. While Steve used lures that he cast out and retrieved, Craig used night crawlers that he put on a hook. He'd cast out as far as he could, allowed his line to fall to the bottom and sat back in his chair holding his rod and waited.

Steve caught three fish in the first hour that passed. A rainbow and two kokanees. Craig spent most of the hour napping. Several times he awoke, changed the worms on his line and continued to nap. Then it happened. He almost lost the rod that he had wedged in the frame of the chair.

The tip of his rod was bent almost forty-five degrees as he set the hook, putting pressure against whatever he had on the other end of his line. He could feel whatever it was tugging on the line. He knew it was big because it was tugging, not the frantic and spastic pulling of a small fish. The fish began to take line off the reel. Steve heard the sound of the reel giving up line and came to Craig's side.

"What cha got boss," he asked.

"Don't know," Craig replied as he strained, keeping pressure on his catch. "It's stopped taking line, but I can't budge it. Don't know if it hung up on something or what."

"Is it still tugging," Steve asked.

"No," Craig answered." It's Just" the spool on the real began screaming as the fish began taking line again. Steve could see that more of the line was exposing itself as he looked out over the water.

"It's coming up boss," he shouted. "Keep the pressure on."

About thirty yards out from the rear of the boat was a large swirl on the water's surface and a large fish rolled and disappeared as it headed down again.

"I think you've got a catfish boss. See if you can start reeling him in toward the boat." Steve was filled with excitement.

Craig began to reel very slowly. It was moving but periodically it would give a big tug and the reel would give up line. After what seemed to be an awful long time Craig had the fish alongside the boat and Steve tried to scope it up in a fish net. It was too heavy, it was a large channel catfish and with Steve using the nets handle and Craig using the ring that the net was threaded on, they both hoisted the fish into the boat. Using a rapala digital fish scale he had in the boats side compartment, Steve found the fish to weigh eleven pounds 10 ounces.

"Congratulations boss," Steve said. "That's a great catch." "That fish wore me out," Craig said, winded from the ordeal.

Steve took a camera from a compartment under the driver's seat and took a picture of Craig with his catch. When holding the fish up with the head chin high, its tail touched the boats deck. Steve hurried with the picture taking so that they could return the fish to the water. They both lifted the fish over the side and gently let it submerge below the water's surface. It just laid motionless for a few moments, so Steve moved it back and forth to make sure water passed through its gills. It finally began to move its tail and with a big thrust it dove out of sight toward the lakes bottom.

Craig sat on the seat at the rear of the boat and recounted to Steve the experience of landing the fish for a few moments, then he became serious.

"Steve," he said. "I've been thinking. I've been thinking that the time may have come for me to hang it up." There was a long silence. Then Craig continued. "The time to begin campaigning for re-election is about here and I'm not sure I should do it. Martha has stood by me all these years. I owe her and times running out. I know I shouldn't care, but I have a concern. Who comes after me?" "I knew that we'd have this conversation eventually Boss," Steve said. "In fact, I've been dreading it. I'm not sure I want to be in the department if you're not there."

The wind had come up a bit and was moving the boat close to the shore. The anchor wasn't holding. He pulled it up. Steve started the engine and slowly moved the boat back to the center of the lake. When he had shut the engine off, he turned so that he was facing Craig.

"Boss," he began. If the sheriffs position becomes vacant and up for grabs, we'll have every wanna be in the county running to be elected. We have some people in the county who have some bizarre ideas about the way this department should be run and what the sheriff's job is."

"Why don't you consider running for the office?" Craig caught Steve by surprise with the question and the conversation was cut short by his beeper going off. He pushed the button that indicated to the call center that he had received the signal and a voice responded.

"SO2, your office needs you to make contact ASAP."

OH, OH Boss! Steve exclaimed. "Looks like things are about to pick up." He reached into the boats glove compartment and took out his assigned radio, that he always had in his possession, keyed the transmit button and began to speak.

"Dispatch, SO2."

"SO2 this is dispatch; Hostage situation at 850 Del Mar Boulevard, Carla's Donuts; two city units on scene; shots fired, officer down; SO6 and SO9 in route." By the time dispatch had finished transmitting, Steve had started the boats engine.

"10-4 Dispatch," Steve said as he eased the boat's throttle forward and it was pushing nose high through the water, gaining speed.

"What's up?" Craig asked.

"Hostage situation at Carla's. What's worse there is an officer down." Steve now had the boat running on top of the water and the wind caused Craig to bend low, close to the windshield, as they made their way to the area where they had launched earlier.

CHAPTER 5

MATT KESSLER WAS on the phone with Pappy Masters discussing future personnel requirements when his emergency line lit up.

"Talk to ya later Pappy," Matt said. "Got a hot call." He hung up on Pappy and punched the blinking red button on phones panel.

"Yeh dispatch, what cha got?"

"Chief, we just got a call from the flower shop on Del Mar Boulevard, Officer Down in front of Carla's donut shop next door," the dispatcher said. "According to Mr. Pearce, owner of the flower shop, someone shot from the donut shop. No one at Carla's is answering the phone. Two of our units and two sheriff's units are in route."

"Advise the fire department of the situation," Matt directed." Have them get a medical response crew over there, also see if they can block off the entrances to the parking lot with their trucks and begin evacuating the area. Who's in charge?" Matt asked.

"Lieutenant Tobias," the dispatcher replied. "Be advised, the Fire Department is in route."

"Have Tobias go to the emergency channel and patch me in," Matt said. He waited nervously until Tobias came on.

Tobias had been with the Police department for more than 18 years. When Matt had become Chief, it was Tobias who acted as his guide

38

when he was familiarizing himself with the city; his sounding board when Matt was accessing the culture of the community, and Tobias was the one who took him around and introduced him to all the officials in the city's government.

Tobias was a big man, tall and imposing. When he entered a room, heads turned. His uniform was impeccable. At one time he had been a body builder. He shaved his head and that added to his imposing appearance.

"Chief, this is Tobias." Matt could hear the pulsating wail of sirens when Tobias transmitted.

"Lieutenant," Matt said. "What's the plan?"

"Get Officer Cranston out of there," Tobias replied. "He's alive. He took one to the lower neck, and is bleeding bad. He made a short transmission and then nothing."

"Keep me posted when you can," Matt asked.

When Tobias arrived on scene the fire trucks had already blocked the entrances. He was advised that crew members were evacuating people out the back doors of each of the stores. One of the city units was parked a good distance in front of the donut shop and an officer was crouched behind the driver's door. He could hear the Sheriff's units as they checked in.

"SO, 6 on scene, positioned at the rear of the donut shop." "SO, 9 In front of the flower shop."

Tobias pulled his car up about 50 feet from the donut shop and he noticed a fire truck moving along the sidewalk in front of the stores. There were four firemen hanging on the side. The truck moved right in front of the door to the donut shop, blocking it. The four firemen jumped off and began attending to officer Cranston. Tobias was positioned so he could see between the fire truck and the door to the shop, so he stood behind his car door and leveled his shot gun at the shop door. Hoping that the perpetrator wouldn't come out using a hostage as a shield. He didn't and the firemen got Cranston in the truck and took him to the far end of the parking lot where they transferred him to an ambulance. One of the firemen was holding an IV bag above his head and another was pumping Cranston's Chest. Tobias turned on his loudspeaker.

"HELLO, IN THE DONUT SHOP- CAN YOU HEAR ME?" His voice over the automobile's loudspeaker could be heard all over the area. He realized that he would get no response from

inside. He had no plan, but he wanted to give the person holding those hostages an opportunity to think about the situation he was in. **"THE BUILDING IS SUROUNDED. I WANT YOU TO THINK ABOUT THAT FOR A WHILE AND I'LL SPEAK TO YOU AGAIN,"** Tobias said. He then picked up his hand radio and spoke to the units in the area.

"Everybody- stay alert," he said. "Remember we have hostages, don't know how many yet. No body fire his weapon unless you're fired upon and you've got a clear shot at the shooter. I repeat, hold your fire unless fired upon. We're gonna try and talk this person out of here without any body getting hurt." As he was giving orders, Steve pulled up, boat still in tow and a flashing red light on top of the truck's cab. Steve pulled his truck right up against the left front quarter panel of Tobias's patrol car. Tobias, Steve and Craig now had great cover from which to operate.

'Hell Sherriff," Tobias said. "Sorry to mess up your fishing trip." "Sure, you are," Craig said. What cha got in there." "Apparently Officer Cranston decided to take a break." Tobias began. "He pulled up in front of the donut shop and as he was walking up to the door someone stuck a gun out the door and shot him."

"How can we be of help to you," Steve asked.

"I need to come up with a way to communicate with somebody in there, "Tobias said.

"I've got an idea," Craig announced. "Over at the corner of the building, by the drug store, is a pay phone. If one of us used it to call the donut shop, we could get a better idea of what we've got."

"A guy would be in the open part way over there," Tobias said. "We could end up with another guy shot." He surveyed the situation. There was a drug store, then a flower shop, the donut shop, a lady's apparel shop, a shoe store and a grocery store on the far end of the mall.

All three stood without speaking for a while. Each contemplating the possibility of using the phone at the end of the building without becoming a target. Craig finally broke the silence.

"Tobias," he said. "Get the phone number of that place from your dispatcher. Whoever shot your officer is not going to open that door with all these units out here. I can get to that phone. It's your call Lieutenant." Even though he could, Craig was not going to take command of the operation from Tobias. They all stood quietly while Tobias mauled over Craig's idea. Then Tobias took out his handheld radio and got the phone number from his dispatcher.

Craig wrote the number in the pad that he always carried in his shirt pocket and began making his way across the parking lot toward the phone. As he was on his way, he reached in his pocket to make sure he had a quarter. He did. Then he realized that he would only get a few minutes with just a quarter. He'd have to get the switchboard at the center of town to give him an open line.

Craig was a member of the area Lions Club, which included Rock Springs and Green River. The District supervisor for the phone company, Martin Cassicks, was also a member. If he could convince the operator to connect him, he may be able to get that open line.

He lifted the receiver from its cradle and the operator said, "Insert twenty-five cents please." He dropped the quarter in the slot, and he heard the dial tone. He dialed "0" and the operator came back on.

"May I help you?" She said.

"Operator, this is Sheriff Spence," Craig began. "I need an open line that I can speak on for an extended time. I know you can't do it on your own so connect me with Mr. Cassicks please."

"One moment Sheriff," she said. It wasn't long before Martin came on the line. Craig explained the situation and Martin Cassicks authorized the open line. When he again got the dial tone, Craig dialed the number to the donut shop.

Craig expected that the person holding the staff hostage would pick up the phone and attempt to negotiate the situation they were in. Surely the sight of all the police cars and fire trucks would give them some angst. The phone rang and rang. Strange Craig thought but wanted to be sure and keep the line open, so he was not going to hang up. Then he got a break. There was the sound of what he thought was someone dropping the receiver on the other end, no one spoke. "Hello," Craig said. No answer. "Hello", Craig said again. "Can you hear me? Hello," Craig continued to try and raise somebody. He tried to imagine what was going on in there. Did someone take the receiver of the cradle so the phone would stop ringing? Did someone take the receiver off its cradle so that what was going on inside could be heard by whoever was listening? Craig cupped the earpiece to keep out any noise. Sure enough, he could hear what sounded like someone breathing heavily. Then he heard a muffled sound. "Mm, UMMM, Ummm, Ummhummhummmmmm!!!"

Craig waved his arm in the air signaling Steve and Lt Tobias to come to his position. When they arrived, he gave the phone to Tobias.

"What does that sound like to you?" Craig asked. "Sounds like someone gaged," Tobias said.

"That's what I thought too, so that indicates to me that whoever was holding the crew hostage isn't with them right now. The question is, where are they?"

Steve took the phone from Tobias and heard the muffled sounds still being made…

Matti Cramer had managed the doughnut shop ever since it opened three years ago. She was a small lady, in her early forties and probably stood five foot six in the flat heeled shoes she always wore. She was legally blind and wore thick lensed glasses with eye ware chords. If they ever fell off, she would never find them.

Nancy, her helper today, was busying herself cleaning the three tables and booths in one corner of the customer area. She was a skinny girl, just out of high school and working part time while waiting to start at the University of Wyoming in Laramie. Matti was putting a tray of fresh backed cake doughnuts in the glass display case when the door opened, and Craven Moss came in.

According to the markings on the door frame, Craven was a little over six foot tall. He had a full head of dirty blond curly hair and a dark brown beard. He always wore military style clothes, pants with lots of pockets and a fatigue jacket with a fourth infantry patch on the shoulder. Matti assumed that he was homeless because he came by almost every day, looking like he needed a bath and smelled like it too. She would give him a couple of day-old doughnuts and a cup of coffee and he would say thanks and be on his way.

Today he appeared to be nervous and his eyes were large and watery. Nancy walk over to him with a couple of doughnuts Matti had given her for him and he grabbed her around the neck and took a handgun out of his jacket pocket. He put the muzzle of the gun behind her ear and yelled at Matti.

"The money!! Give it to me!!" Matti stood stunned but kept her cool.

"It's been a slow day," she said. "There ain't much."

Craven dragged Nancy behind the counter and forced both women to get on their knees. He took a roll of duct tape from one of his pants pockets and handed it to Nancy. He instructed her to tape Matti's hands at the wrists and legs at the ankles. When she finished, he then taped her hands and legs. He also placed tape across the mouths of both women. He was trying to open the cash register when he saw a police car pull up in front of the shop. He ran to the door and when the officer began walking toward the shop, Craven opened the door and shot.

He then ran back to the register, but he couldn't get it to open. Panicking, he began looking for a way out. He tried escaping through the back door, but it was locked. He was looking for a key in the drawers behind the counter when the fire trucks began arriving in the parking lot, lights flashing and sirens blaring.

Matti watched him go into a small storage room where she kept her supplies, paper cups, napkins etc. She heard him moving boxes and then she heard the door to the storage room close. She scooted across the floor to where Nancy was sitting and positioned herself so that they were back to back. Matti tried using her fingers, which she could move, to pull the tape off Nancy's hands. She was still trying to find the end of the tape when the phone on the wall began to ring. At first, she just stared at it. Then she rolled until she was under the phone. She managed to get on her knees and using the wall for support, stood up and used her head to knock the receiver from its cradle. In the process she knocked her glasses off and couldn't see where the receiver was. Nancy, seeing her dilemma, rolled over and began making noises into receiver that was hanging by its chord, very close to the floor…

"Tobias," Steve said. "I don't believe our guy is there anymore. If he were, I don't believe he'd let what's happening, happen. I think we need to get in there."

Tobias took out his radio and contacted units on surveillance. "All units at the doughnut shop, stay alert," he said. "We're going in."

On their hands and knees, they began to make their way along the base of the buildings outside wall. Tobias led the way, staying below the window and close against the wall, followed by Steve and Craig bringing up the rear.

When he reached the door to the shop, Tobias stood up, pressing his shoulder against the brick wall between the window and the door. Steve went past him and stood up facing Tobias. He could see into the shop. He could see most of the room but saw no one. He advised Tobias that he could see no one. Tobias reached out and opened the door enough to get his foot between it and the frame.

"Police," he said in a loud voice. **"The games over, come out with your hands up."** There was no response, but they could hear what sounded like the same muffled sounds they'd heard over the phone only this time the sounds were more frantic.

"Steve," Tobias said. "You pull this door open and I'm going to dive in. Sheriff, would you cover me please?" As if each man was on a timer, they moved in unison. Steve yanked the door open and Tobias dove into the room and rolled across the floor toward the back of the shop. Craig was right behind him and crashed up against the counter. Steve dove over the counter and landed right on top of Matti who let out a high-pitched shriek through her nose.

"Looks like the place is clear," Craig said as he retrieved his hat that had gone flying across the room when he hit the counter. Steve sat Matti up against the wall and peeled the tape off her mouth.

"Where is he?" Steve asked.

"He went in the storeroom," Matti said nodding with her head at the door close to where Tobias was standing. He turned and stood against the wall behind the door so that if it opened, he'd be able to slam it shut. Craig laid his arms across the counter and leveled the shot gun he'd taken from Tobias at the phone booth, at the storeroom door. Steve busied himself removing the tape from the women and moving them out of the field of fire.

"You're trapped," Tobias shouted. **"No one needs to get hurt. Knock on the door and let me know you want to come out."** There was no response. Tobias changed his position so he could open the door without exposing himself.

"Sheriff," he said. I'm going to open this door. Use that scatter gun if he comes out shooten."

When the door flew open it banged against the wall and that was the only sound for several minutes. Tobias peeked into the storeroom He could see several boxes stacked in the middle of floor in a room that was otherwise neatly organized. The boxes were out of place.

He looked up and noticed that a panel in the false ceiling was gone and was laying on the floor beside the boxes.

"Christ!!" Tobias Exclaimed. "He's in the rafters!"

A pin could have been heard had it dropped. No one moved except eyes surveying the ceiling above them. Craig was the first to speak.

"I'm going to get these women out of here." Slowly he moved along the wall still watching the ceiling. He signaled to Mattie and Nancy, who were sitting in a booth, to come to him. He took them outside. Once they were away from the building a safe distance, he began to quiz them.

"Did you know the person that's in there?"

"Yeh, Mattie spoke up. "His name is Craven, Craven Moss. I think he's homeless. He came in the first time about a month ago, said he was hungry, and I gave him a couple of day-old doughnuts and he left. Since then he's come in almost every day. I don't know when he told me his name but somewhere along the line he did. I never thought he'd do something like this."

"You think he's on drugs," Craig asked.

"I don't know," Mattie said shrugging her shoulders. "His eyes looked a little weird today, but I wouldn't know if he was or not."

"Did he say anything when he came in," Craig pushed on. "After he grabbed Nancy he just said, "The money, give me the

money."

"OK, you two go over to that police car where the boat is and stick around. I'm sure the police officer will want to talk to you some more." Craig returned to the doughnut shop.

"Saw you talking to the ladies," Tobias said. "Anything we can use?"

'Yep," Craig said. "His name is Craven, and he's probably homeless."
"Hell Sheriff," Tobias began. "He could be anywhere in this complex. Got any ideas how we can flush him out?"

"You may be in luck, Lieutenant," Craig said. "I happened to have been present when the county Fire Chief told the construction companies lawyers how the construction had to go. I was at the meeting because there was a group of people protesting the building of this Mall. One of the requirements was that the building be flat topped. The other was that every cinder block wall between shop spaces had to go all the way to the flat roof forming a fire wall between shops. Your man is trapped between the flower shop and the ladies store next door. He is somewhere above the false ceiling in this store, and he's standing on very narrow footing. I think you might be able to talk him down."

"OK Craven," Tobias said in a loud voice. **"We know you're up there. We also know you're trapped. You've made a mistake and you don't want to make matters worse. We don't want to hurt you. Why don't you just come on down and let's get this thing over with?"**

"Why should I trust you?" The voice was weak and forlorn. Steve moved over where he thought the sound was coming from. And pointed to the spot where he felt Craven was.

"We know where you are Craven," Tobias said. **"We could have blasted you out of there with a shot gun some time ago. We didn't because we promised that we didn't want to hurt you. Why did you do this anyway?"**

"I needed the money," Craven said.

"Are you homeless," Tobias asked.

"Lost my job as a truck driver six months ago. We were evicted from our apartment three months ago. My wife, Karen has MS and we've run out of her medicine. I didn't know what else to do."

"Where have you been living?" Tobias continued to press. "In our car that I park at the rest stop east of town at night," was the reply.

"What makes you think your being dead is going to help your wife?"

Tobias asked. "You've made a lot of bad decisions today Craven. Don't make another one, come down," Tobias said. There was silence. All the lawmen waited for several minutes, then Craig spoke up.

"Craven, this is sheriff Spence. Your wife needs help. I'll make you a promise. Take out that ceiling panel right in front of you, drop your weapon down, we'll then help you down and I promise that I'll see to it that your wife gets the help she needs. You're running out of time son. We're going to end this stand off and the odds are not in your favor." Again, they waited. Tobias spoke to Craig.

"Since we know where he is. I'm going to see if the fire chief will bring one of his trucks over here and we'll blast his ass out of there with a fire hose and if he fires that gun, he's a dead man."

"No," Craig said pointing at the ceiling. "Look at that." The panel was moving. When it had been taken out a hand appeared with small handgun, a revolver, and the gun was dropped to the floor. Tobias picked it up and pushed the plunger that expelled the bullets. Two feet appeared and as promised, Craig and Steve grabbed the legs attached to them and slowly lowered Craven. Steve immediately applied cuffs and had Craven sit on the floor.

"Where is your wife," Craig asked.

"About two blocks up the street in the car, a 1979 tan ford Galaxy," Craven said. "She may be sleeping, she scares easy, Please. let me go with you, it will be best if I wake her."

"Are there any weapons in the car?" Tobias asked.

"Yeh," Craven said hesitantly. "Whenever I'm not there she has a 22 pistol under her pillow or under the covers she has over her."

Tobias got on his radio and gave the other officers the all clear and advised that the suspect was in custody. He also thanked the fire chief for the help that his men had given and asked that he have an ambulance stand by.

After placing Craven in his car, Craig and Steve got in and went with Tobias to where Cravens car was located. Tobias allowed Craven to approach the car while Tobias held on to the cuffs on his hands behind his back.

On the back seat of the car was a pile of blankets and Steve, who had gone around to the opposite side of the car, could see the head of a female sticking from under the pile. He signaled Tobias that someone was there. Tobias reached around Craven and tapped on the window. The covers rolled back, and the woman sat up.

"Open the door sweetheart," Craven said. She unlocked and opened the door. Tobias saw that there was no weapon in her hands. He passed Craven to Craig and reached in and took the woman by the arm. She screamed and tried to pull away. Tobias pulled her out of the vehicle and stood her against the car. She was a pitiful little thing. Thin, pale, and having difficulty coordinating the movements of her limbs.

"It's okay baby," Craven was saying. "Where's the gun," Tobias asked.

"It's under the pillow," the woman said in a whimpering voice. "What's going on?"

"I did something stupid honey," Craven said. "I tried to get some money so we could get your medicine. I panicked and shot a cop." Tobias grabbed Craven by the collar and admonished him.

"Hush!" Tobias shouted. He continued to advise Craven of his rights. In the excitement he had neglected to do it earlier.

"No," she said, putting her hand to her mouth. "You didn't do that. Oh God I just want to die, It's all my fault. I just want to die." Craig moved close to her and tried to calm her down. He explained that Craven had made some bad decisions but that his office would see that she got the help she needed while her husband dealt with his situation. His comments didn't seem to mean much to her.

With Craig and Steve in the back seat and Craven between them, Tobias put the wife in the passenger seat and headed back to the parking lot where the ambulance was waiting. Craig used Steve's radio to give instructions to his office. He directed that CPI be notified that he was detaining a female and she would be transported to the hospital. He would meet them there after he'd made the appropriate arrangements.

Tobias, in the meantime was on his radio briefing the Chief of Police as he was transporting Craven to the city jail. During the conversation Matt had advised him that off duty officers from the police department and sheriff's office had given blood and officer Cranston, though in critical condition, had a good chance of making it.

Martha picked up the newspaper as she was on her way to the kitchen to Join Craig, who had already prepared two cups of coffee and was sitting at the table awaiting her entrance.

"Morning Doll," he greeted her. "How goes it today?"

"You Know," she started as she placed the paper on the table in front of him. "I think I might make it through the day. I'm beginning to feel like myself again. When you came home last night, you didn't tell me you had been out playing cops and robbers all day. I thought you were fishing."

"Where'd you hear that," he asked.

"Look at the headlines," She said. Craig picked up the paper as he took a sip out of his coffee. Across the front page in large bold letters was: **"SWEETWATER COUNTY SHERIFF CRAIG SPENCE AND SEVERAL SHERIFFSDEPUTIES, TEAM UP WITH ROCKSPRINGS POLICE AND FIRE DEPARTMENT, TO CAPTURE DOUGHNUT SHOP ROBBER."**

"We were out on the lake when we got a call on the radio that there was a hostage situation," Craig began. "We had pretty much finished fishing. I'd caught a big old catfish. We put him back and was just relaxing and talking when we got the call." Craig proceeded to fill Martha in on what had taken place and the sorry situation Craven, and his wife were in.

"Poor dear," Martha said with a sigh. "I'm sure the young man was taken to jail, but what did you do with her, she didn't do anything wrong?"

"I had her put in detention. She appeared to be in bad shape. At least she'll be able to get some of the meds she needs."

"You old softy," Martha chided.

"The police department is gonna want to talk to her anyway and they'll know where to find her."

CHAPTER 6

MATT KESSLER, ROCK Springs Police Chief, had suffered the results of no secretary for a month or so when he knew he had to make a change. He had taken Maggie, who had been his secretary from the day he started, and put her in the community assistance pool because she had violated his trust by being an informant regarding police activities. He couldn't replace her because he hadn't gone through the disciplinary process of demoting her out of the position or firing her. He also knew that he had put the city in a bad legal position if Maggie decided to file a complaint about the actions he had taken in this matter.

His handling of correspondence was horrible and reports to the other agencies were always late because he didn't know what was due until people called to inquire. Thank goodness Maggie had a list of reports required under the glass on her desk. She also had copies of previous reports in the files, so he was able to produce updated copies. This had to stop, he thought. People are constantly asking why Maggie wasn't at her desk and he was running out of reasons, plus all his time was taken up doing paperwork and answering the phone. What a conundrum, he was thinking.

At the end of the day, when everyone was preparing to leave for the day, Matt walked over to the Community Assistance area and saw that Maggie too was preparing to leave. As he watched, he realized that he had never really seen Maggie before. She was quite attractive with her dark, almost black, hair that fell well below her shoulders; matched her dark eyes that set wide apart under thin trimmed eyebrows; even though she was rather short in stature she had a royal posture.

As he entered the room she looked up in his direction as she was picking up her purse from the desk. With his finger he beckoned to her to follow him and he walked back toward his office. He looked once over his shoulder to make sure she was following, and she was. Once at his desk he motioned her to take a seat, in the same chair that she used to use when she was taking notes or dictation.

"How are you doing over there in the CA department?" he asked in order to get the conversation started.

"I'm surviving Matt," she responded. "I realize I have a debt to pay for what I did. I'm just thankful that you were kind enough not to fire me, I like working here and I need the job."

"Well," Matt began. "I think we've both been punished considerably by it all."

"I'm sorry, I guess I don't understand," Maggie said with a frown on her face.

"I should have fired you. Instead I let my soft side get in the way. In my anger I knew I had to punish you though, and I moved you over to the most menial job that I could think of. In doing so I punished myself too. I haven't been able to function worth a darn around here, and this place is a mess without you. No one knows about what happened except you, me and the audio technician that alerted me and he's a contractor. Don't expected him to care one way or the other. I'm putting you back at your desk."

For a minute they both just sat and looked at each other. Then Maggie could no longer constrain herself. She jumped up, dropping her purse to the floor, ran around the desk and threw her arms around Matt. The chair that he was sitting in was the type that would swivel, and the back support would rotate back. The force of Maggie's charge caused the chair to rotate backwards, the chair tipped over and they both ended up on the floor in a disheveled bundle. Once they got over the shock of it, and realized what they must have looked like, they lay there laughing.

Matt was the first to get himself together and helped Maggie to her feet. Once they were reseated in their chairs, Matt continued the conversation.

"What's the status of your husband's obligation to the people at the Silver Dollar," he asked.

"If you're not aware, the place sold," she said. "According to an acquaintance that is going to work for the new owners, all of the old cadre is gone to the four winds. The old company has been completely disbanded."

"That should relieve the strain off you guys," Matt stated. "When I realized that there was no longer a reason to be

fearful," Maggie began. "It was like the whole world was lifted off my shoulders. I began to realize what this entire situation with his gambling had cost us. Our lives had been ripped apart. We were in constant fear that they would find some way to make us pay up or otherwise compensate them for the debt. It had cost me my job and my reputation, everything that I'd worked for. I cried when they told me that all our persecutors were gone. Then I went home and confronted Ernest. I told him That I felt that I had done my part. I'd stuck with him through his ordeal, been humiliated and reduced to the threat of becoming a prostitute or worse. I told him that I had no reason to believe that he understood how devastating it was for me to have to do what I did to this department, nor did I have any reason to believe that he wouldn't continue gambling and put us in a like situation again. We've been separated for a little over three weeks and I've seen an attorney to start divorce proceedings."

"Gees, I'm really sorry things turned out this way," Matt said. "No, don't be," Maggie replied. "Now that it has happened,

I realize that the love and respect in the marriage was one sided anyway. I hit bottom and now that you've been kind enough to give me a second chance, there's no way but up. I thank you from the bottom of my heart Mr. Kessler."

"You'd better get out of here," Matt said. "I don't want you blaming me for having to work overtime."

Maggie picked up her purse from the floor and headed to the door. Just as she was about to enter the outer office, she heard Matt call out.

"Hey Maggie," he shouted. "As before, Matt will do."

Several weeks past and with Maggie back at her desk the department was running like a well-oiled machine again. The other city department heads were off his back about late reports and the quality of correspondence and such, so he had time for other stuff like the Silver Spur.

One afternoon Maggie called on the intercom to let Matt know that there was a gentleman who said his name was Jeff Flores waiting to see him. Matt hadn't seen Jeff since the original meeting regarding the change in ownership and operations at the Silver spur and Wagon Wheel.

"Yeh, send him in," Matt said. Jeff sauntered in holding his battered cowboy hat against his chest, a toothpick sticking out the side of his mouth and he had a bruise along the side of his head just behind his left eye. In fact, Matt noticed that the eye was a bit swollen.

"Good to see you Jeff," Matt said as he motioned for the cowboy to take a seat. "You look like somebody disagreed with you."

"What's that?" Jeff inquired, not getting what Matt was referring to.

"That swelling and bruise alongside your head," Matt explained. "Oh that," Jeff said, waving his arm dismissing the idea that he had been in a fight. "I was trying to take a rock out of my horse's hoof, and he took offense. I didn't duck fast enough."

"Guess you might say there was a misunderstanding, huh?" Matt said with a grin on his face. "You heard anything interesting happening at the Silver Spur? I haven't been paying any attention and there's been no complaints."

"No, not really," Jeff responded. "There is something that's been eaten at me though. A couple of weeks before the construction was finished over there, I saw a truck deliver steel girders, you know the type that would be used to support an upper floor."

Matt thought about what Jeff had said for a moment and then as though thinking out loud replied.

"That place has always been one level, I think. We never got any body on the inside to keep us posted about what was going on. I'll call Craig and see if they have anything. Thanks for coming by Jeff. I'll follow up and see what's going on." With that Jeff got up, gave a thumbs up sign and walked out into the outer office.

Craig had just returned from having lunch with Martha and fortunately was in his office when Matt called. He had been looking over deputy's reports from the night before. He let the phone ring a couple of times before he answered.

"Spence here," he said.

"Hey Craig," Matt said. "Wasn't sure I'd catch ya. How goes it?" "Like I like it-Slow," Craig said. "How about you?"

"I just finished talking to Jeff Flores," Matt began. "He's telling me that he saw a load of steel girders over at the Silver Spur a couple of weeks ago, the type that could be used to support an upper floor. Your guys report anything out of the ordinary going on over there?" "No," Craig replied. "You think maybe they put in a basement?

I'll check with Kevin. He's the one that's been keeping an eye out. I'll get back with you."

"Thanks Craig, and by the way, haven't talked to you for a while, thanks for your help on that attempted robbery at the Doughnut shop."

"Wasn't aware that your phone lines were down all these weeks, but I accept the belated courtesy," Craig needled Matt. "Just joking Chief. You're very welcome." After hanging up, Craig used the intercom to call Kevin to his office. When he walked in Craig chastised him.

"In the last couple of weeks, you haven't said a word about the Silver Spur situation. You been keeping an eye on things over there?" "Yeh Sheriff, and I was hoping to have something concrete for you."

"What's going on," Craig asked.

"I haven't really seen anything out of the ordinary," Kevin said. "They did build a covered walkway up to a new doorway behind the building. I didn't think that was anything out of the ordinary." "Jeff Flores said that he had seen some steel girders on a truck over there. You see anything like that?" Craig asked. "No," Kevin said.

"The only use for those girders would be to support some type of structure or to shore up something. Go to the city building inspectors and see what they can tell you about the remodeling of that building," Craig commented. "Get back to me as soon as you can."

Following Craig's direction, Kevin went to the Rock Springs City Building Inspectors office and sat down with an inspector over a set of plans representing the remodeling of the Silver Spike building. There were two different large sheets and Kevin had no idea what they showed.

The inspector was very helpful in explaining what the plans displayed. He started with the sheet marked with the number 1, and stamped, **MAIN FLOOR** under the name and address of the building.

"This is the layout of the changes and additions to the main floor," the Inspector began. "There were the additions at the rear entrance area and the relocation of the plumbing to the men's and women's bathrooms in both the club area and restaurant. Because they were back to back, the plumbing was through the same channels down into the basement."

"There is a basement in that building?" Kevin asked.

"Oh yes," the inspector replied. "Initially there was a furnace down there, a large water tank, and an electric operated pump that pumped water from a well. The rest of the full basement had been used for storage and a maintenance shop."

"How did you get down into the basement?" Kevin asked and the inspector took out the second sheet marked with the number 2.

Pointing to an area on the sheet that the Inspector identified as the rear entrance, he showed the location of a staircase in an area marked, **STOREROOM** and he also pointed to another room **MARKED OFFICE** on another section of the sheet that showed a staircase to the basement. He then pointed to an area across from the storeroom marked **COAT ROOM** and stated that along with the rear entrance these were the additions to the main floor. He then pointed out that there had been three areas added to the basement that each were marked as a **G ROOM.** The Inspector also showed Kevin where all the electrical and phone boxes were located.

Kevin pointed to a dark line that ran beyond the Coat room and the Storeroom and asked:

"What is this line that crosses here?"

"That's a wall that separates that area from the club. It is actually at the end of the hall that leads to the club's bathrooms."

"So," Kevin inquired. "If you enter through the rear entrance, you can't get into the club or the restaurant, but you could enter the storeroom where the stairs to the basement are?"

"That appears to be true," affirmed the Inspector.

"Is it possible to get a copy of these plans," Kevin asked.

"I don't see why not," the Inspector said." I'll make you a copy.

You'll have to sign our log showing who has copies." "Not a problem," Kevin said.

CHAPTER 7

WHEN CRAIG ENTERED the conference room for the morning meeting, only Steve and Sherrie were there. When Craig sat down in his chair at the head of the table Steve spoke up.

"Kevin just ran out. Said he had to get something out of his car for the meeting."

Hearing this, Craig relaxed, took hIs hat and laid it on the table in front of him. He ran his fingers through his thinning hair and spoke to Steve.

"You know," he began. "The other day when we were out in the boat, I was just getting to enjoy it when we had to leave. When you gonna do that again?"

"Don't know Boss. I'll have to see if I can interest the gentleman, I work for to let me steal away." Craig let a smile cross his face and responded.

"The gentleman you work for could really get used to that kind of activity," and they both chuckled as Kevin came into the room carrying a roll of large paper sheets.

"Okay," Craig said. "Now that we're all here I guess we can get started." Kevin laid the roll on the table and said to Craig.

"You're going to be glad I went after this stuff Sheriff." "Alright," Craig said and then he continued. "Sherrie, did we ever get reimbursed for taking Paul to Arizona?"

"I got paperwork a couple of days ago authorizing Sweetwater County to submit a bill to Maricopa County to cover the cost of transporting Paul," Sherrie replied. "I took it over to the Treasurer's Office and they sent it out. I doubt if they've gotten a check yet."

"When we get the bill from CPI make sure we send in a transfer request so that the money is credited to our account," Craig directed.

"Will do," Sherrie assured him.

"What can you tell me about the wife of that young man who tried to rob the doughnut shop in Rock Springs?"

"Her name was Nancy, Nancy Moss," Sherrie replied. "The hospital's Patient Coordinators Office managed to get her enrolled in a Multiple Sclerosis study project in Cheyenne, Wyoming and she was transferred to a clinic up there. We also got an order from County Court, to release Craven to the Larimar County Sheriff's Office, that's the county that Cheyenne is in. His case was transferred there, and he would serve any sentence he receives up there for what he tried to do. Looks like the officer is going to survive. That would put him near his wife. I don't know who went to bat for him."

"I don't think it matters," Craig said. "I think the outcome is probably the best all-around. What else you got?"

"We have an elderly man, he's in his 80's," Sherrie started." He's in lock up at the hospital. He suffers from Alzheimer's and he tries to beat on his wife who is his care giver. She finally had to call the police for help. The police thought it would be safest for all concerned if he was detained until a suitable place could be found where he could be taken care of."

"What about him going after the nurses and guards up there," Craig asked.

"Apparently he's as nice as pie to everyone but as soon as his wife shows up, he goes after her," Sherrie said. "That's all I have Sheriff." "Steve," Craig inquired. "You got anything that's keeping you busy?"

"Yeah Boss," Steve began. "You remember Kevin was going to try and find the stuff in his boxes pertaining to that Mr. Costello? Well he brought the boxes in and I helped him go through them, and we found what we were looking for. The BOLO that was out on this guy was out of Montana. He was being investigated for running an illegal gambling operation and he split before they could question him. We notified the Montana State Criminal guys that we had him and they came and got him. I checked with Montana and Costello ended up spending six months in jail and a year on probation."

"And he's now the general manager for this new operation at the Silver Spur?" Craig expounded.

"Yep," Steve replied. "I think there's an ill wind blowing." With that having been said, Kevin spoke up.

"If you remember Sheriff, the other day you asked me to check with the Rock Springs City Building Inspectors about the remodeling going on at the Silver Spur. Well, I did." As he spoke, Kevin rolled out the plans in front of Craig and when Steve and Sherrie had gathered around, proceeded to explain what the building inspector had told him the drawings represented. When he had finished Craig pointed to the staircase leading to the basement from the storeroom and said. "Looking at the area where the stairs are, there's a large open area and the footage indicated on the plans shows it to be forty-two feet in length and sixteen feet wide. I wonder what they have planned for it?" Craig then pointed to the area marked G Rooms and thought aloud. "My devious mind tells me that these rooms may have specific uses planned for them."

The four of them poured over the plans Kevin had brought for almost an hour and each expressed their best guess as to what was going to go on in the basement of that building. Then Craig broke up the gathering.

"I'm going to show these plans to the Chief in Rock Springs. I don't think we've ever had this type of a heads up on a potential operation before. I'll call him and have him come here. He had a problem with someone leaking information not too long ago. Good Work Kevin. Anybody got anything else?"

"I've got something," Sherrie said. "We've got just a little over a year before we have to start campaigning. Are you going to run for office again Sheriff?"

"When I know, you'll be the first to know," Craig said. "Let's get this day started." Craig got up, put his hat on and strode out of the room.

It was late in the day when Matt Kessler arrived at Craig's office. He had Maggie in tow. After he received Craig's call, he realized that he'd better start documenting the meetings regarding the Silver Spur caper. Craig and Kevin were in the office. The large sheets that Kevin had gotten at the City Building Inspectors office, covered Craig's desk. Matt and Maggie took seats in front of the desk while Kevin stood so he could reach all the respective sections of the plans. After Matt introduced Maggie to Craig and Kevin, he explained why he had brought her along.

"When you told me why you wanted us to meet, it finally dawned on me that if this ever turned into a case, we'd need documentation of the steps we took in order to bring a case in the first place and to show probable cause. So, I brought Maggie here with me to begin that process. I'd suggest that you guys do the same."

"I've already started a file of my reports regarding this matter from the day we held our first meeting," Kevin spoke up. "I'd be glad to get with Maggie at her convenience and bring her up to date."

"I'd appreciate that," Maggie said.

It took a little over an hour for Kevin to explain what was depicted on the plans, answer the questions that Matt asked and give an overview of what he thought was going on or what would happen in the future. Matt then added something that added to the growing puzzle.

"One of my patrol people was shaking doors a few weeks ago," Matt began. "He drove around behind the Silver Spur and decided to check that door that had been put in back there. There is a key card required to get in that door. So, obviously that entrance is not for the run of the mill customer. Since, according to the plans, there is no passageway to the club or restaurant, and there is a coat room just inside that door, I'd bet that storage room is more than just a storage room."

"I just noticed something," Craig said pointing to a part of the plan marked number one. "It's almost lost in all the lines that show plumbing and wiring routes in the kitchen. There's another door leading to the outside of the building. I wonder if that has a key card lock. They've got to have some way of getting the trash and stuff out, I'll bet that's it."

"I'll check with my people and see what's back there," Matt said. "Also," Craig continued. The parking lot extends back there where the covered entrance is. Could you have your people start checking license plates? I'd be interested in what out of county and regulars that park back there."

"Great idea," Matt affirmed. "We'll do it."

"While you're here Maggie," Kevin inquired. "Why don't you come with me and I'll make copies of my file for you and you can take them to your office and add them to your packet." Matt motioned for her to go ahead.

The trip to the Detective's Department for information related to the Silver Spur, produced more than copies of Kevin's files. While he and Maggie waited for the copies to spurt out of the machine they engaged in small talk until finally Kevin made the conversation a little more personal.

"What do you do for entertainment Maggie?" He asked. Maggie noticed that the copies were ready.

"The copies are ready." She said. "Why? What did you have in mind?"

"Well," Kevin began. "I noticed that there is an indication on your ring finger that there was a ring there once. Looks like it was just recently removed. I live an uneventful life outside the office. Thought maybe we could have dinner sometime." Holding out her hand and looking at the circular indent in her finger Maggie spoke with some sadness in her voice.

"I guess your past leaves an imprint in more ways than one. I'm currently going through a divorce. After work I spend a lot of time reading and wishing things were not the way they are." Maggie took the copies from Kevin and continued speaking. "I'm not much fun these days, but you know where to find me. Give me a call sometime and we'll see."

After showing Maggie back to Craig's office Kevin stood watching as Matt and Maggie walked toward their car. Just before Maggie got in the car, she looked back at Kevin and smiled.

Conversation was sparse at the Spence supper table today. Craig had gotten home a bit late and Martha and Katie were already eating when he got there. Craig just assumed that his late arrival didn't set well with the two of them. Kraut Burgers were on the menu tonight and Craig had eaten two and was starting on his third when Martha broke the silence.

"Katie has something she needs to tell you." "You're mad at me for being late," Craig piped up.

"No," Martha said. "I'm the one that is a little miffed at the burgers getting cold while we waited for you, she has something much more important to say."

"Well Katie," Craig said. "What's on your mind?" Katie wiped her mouth with her napkin, sat up straight in her chair and dropped her bomb.

"I'm leaving," she announced. There was a moment of silence while Craig cleared his mouth of burger before he spoke.

"Leaving," he said. "what does that mean? Leaving where?" "Which question do you want me to answer first," Katie quipped. "All of them, dognapped," Craig raised his voice a little. "What do you mean you're leaving?"

"I've been offered a job as a care giver for an elderly lady in Thermopolis, dad." No one spoke. Martha stopped chewing and stared down at the Burger on her plate. Katie sat looking Craig straight in the eye with a look of anxiety in her own and a frown on her brow. She spoke.

"I won't be leaving right away," she said. "The person who has the job now won't be leaving until next month." Craig sat motionless, as if he had been frozen in place. Katie spoke again.

"I really need to do this, dad. Mom doesn't need me anymore and I need to get a life."

"I was just thinking," Craig began. "I was just thinking how great it's been having you here with us all these months. We love you kitten." Katie hadn't heard her dad call her that since she was in kindergarten. Tears began to flow from Martha's eyes and Katie jumped up and ran around the table to hug her dad.

"How did you manage to get a job in Thermopolis," Craig inquired.

"you know I've been taking Mom to her appointments," Katie began to explain. "All the offices have magazines on the tables in the waiting rooms and I would browse through them. One day I ran across an ad for a care giver in one of them and I thought, why not. I wrote a letter and a couple of days ago I got a call and this nurse interviewed me over the phone. She talked to Mom too. We hung up and we didn't think anything would come of it. Well, today she called back and offered me the job. I have to let her know before noon tomorrow."

"Go for it Katie," Craig said. I'm happy for you. Your mother and I will be just fine."

"Now that you've managed to make us both cry," Martha interjected. "You need to hear what else she has to say."

"You mean there's more," Craig asked.

"Dad," Katie started. "You are into the second year of your fourth term as sheriff. When you get into the third year, you'll have to begin forming a campaign strategy for re-election. Tell me, are you going to run for re-election? Craig sat back in his chair and crossed his arms across his chest. He took a moment before he responded.

"You're the second person who has asked me that today," he said. "I've given it some thought but haven't really decided." Katie pressed on.

"If you run," She started. "It's unlikely but possible, that you could lose. If that should happen, you and Mom will have to leave this house. Where will you go? Will you rent an apartment some place? What will you do? The situation is the same for you and Mom if you decide not to run. I'm not going to be here, and I need to know that you and Mom are going to be alright."

"You make a good argument Katie," Craig admitted. There are some things I need to consider." Craig put his elbows on the table and cradled his head in his hands. Martha placed her hand on his arm and asked:

"Love," she said. "Why is it so hard to make this decision? You make decisions for people every day. What is it?" Craig put his arm around Martha, pulled her close and put his chin on top of her head and spoke very softly, as if speaking to himself.

"Other than my stint in the Navy, being involved with law enforcement has been my life. It's something I'm pretty good at, I've been useful, I've contributed and made some people's lives better, and some worse, but I've been the captain of my own ship, sort of. What do I do after. That's what I've been struggling with. What do I do?" "You'll be a pain in the butt," Martha said as she pulled away so she could look at his face. "For a while you'll pace like a caged lion; then you'll go fishing; you'll have coffee in the mornings with friends you've made over the years; we'll do things together that we've never been able to do all these years. If you don't give it up, we'll keep right on living day to day like we always have. You need to decide which sounds better."

"Dad," Katie broke in. "I've got a suggestion. There are some real neat retirement communities in Cheyenne, Cody, Laramie, Sheridan - a lot of nice places in Wyoming if you want to stay here. You and Mom could live in one of these places without any worries at all. Before I leave, why don't you let me drive you and Mom to look at some of these. We could do one or two ever weekend."

"I've never considered living in those places," said Craig. "I've wondered if they were like nursing homes."

"Will you let me show you one?" Katie pressed. "In the meantime, what are you going to do about campaigning for another term as Sheriff?"

"You know," Craig began. "I've always wanted to take a cruise. When I was in the Navy, we spent a lot of time at sea, but I didn't see any places, and I would like to take a fishing trip to Alaska. If we were to take a cruise doll, where would you like to go?"

"Jamaica. Australia. Greece – all over," Martha said.

"There's one other thing I'd like to get done before I quit," Craig announced. "I wanna move the department into a new facility. If that happens during this term, I know time is short, so even if the New building is authorized during this term, I'll not campaign. In the meantime, Katie, I'll let you show us what these retirement places have to offer. Fair enough."

"Not exactly what I wanted to hear" Katie said with a sigh. "but I understand."

"What's the status of that project anyway," Martha asked. "With any luck," Craig said, crossing his fingers. "The

Commissioners will have the first vote at this month's meeting."

Days turned into weeks and weeks turned into a couple of months. Enforcement requirements were routine, and the Silver Spur became the place to eat out and the best entertainment in town on the weekend. Family dinning was featured during the week and a sports bar boomed on Friday and Saturday as patrons watched their favorite college and professional sports teams.

According to license plates in the parking lot, people were coming from all the surrounding counties on Friday and Saturday nights. As far as the enforcement community could tell, everything was on the up and up and the Silver Spur was an asset to the entire county. People from the departments who conducted surveillance from time to time could identify no laws that were being broken. They had been unsuccessful in finding a way to get into the lower level, the renovated basement, because the outside entrance required a card key and the only other access was through the office and administrative portion of the business which was always manned. There was a more pressing problem that Pappy Masters was making Mat aware of.

"I've been using one of my crew to monitor what is happening over at the Spur," Pappy was saying to Matt as they sipped coffee in the department's break room. "Some of the patrolmen who have eaten over there told me that they've seen my guy cozying up to the night manager when they've been there. The night manager I understand is pretty sexy. I'm concerned that my guy might be thinking with the wrong head."

"You haven't confronted hm about it," Matt asked.

"There might be nothing to it," replied Pappy. "I wanted to run the situation by you and see what you thought."

"Why don't you get with him and see what's going on, Matt advised. We don't have to be too concerned about him passing on any plans or suspicions, because we don't have any. We suspect that there is gaming going on over there, there might even be prostitution based on what we know about the way the renovated basement is configured, but we have no proof of it. The place is probably being run as a private club and as long as there is no complaint from anyone, I'm prepared to just sit on the information we have, it could come in handy later, and keep an eye on the place."

"Okay, Pappy agreed. I'm planning on having dinner over there tonight, I'll talk to him then if he's there."

"Mind if I join you?" Matt asked.

"Not at all, meet you there about 6:30," Pappy said.

The entrance to the Silver Spur opened into a vestibule, where hostess greeted all customers. There were two doors, one on the left that opened into the bar and one on the right that gave entry to the restaurant. Matt advised the hostess that he was to meet someone in the restaurant, and she moved ahead of him with an arm full of menus and his silver ware. He was a little early and he didn't see Pappy anywhere.

The room was quite large with indirect lighting provided by shaded lights positioned strategically along the walls. There were tables with four to six chairs in the center of the room and booths along the walls. There were murals of western scenes, Cowboys on horseback, and cattle being rounded up in a valley appearing to be positioned to cross a river.

Waiters and waitresses moved swiftly among the tables and booths, some carrying large trays of food and others pouring coffee or delivering other beverages. Matt pointed to a booth in which he'd like to sit, and the hostess escorted him to it. As he was being seated Pappy came over and slid into the seat across from Matt.

"I got here a little early," Pappy said." I had time to visit with my guy in the bar for a bit."

"Has this officer been in your department for a while or is he someone that has just transferred in recently?" Matt was curious.

"It's Jim Crawford," Pappy advised. "He just moved over from patrol a couple of months ago. I thought he'd be best over here because the old guys are too well known. Just so happens that the night manager here is Jim's wife's cousin. He assured me that she's cool and has been a great source of information about the place.

"What has he found out?" Matt asked. Before Pappy could answer a waitress stopped to ask for their order. They hadn't looked at the menu, but both had heard that the prime rib dinner was good so they both ordered it. After the waitress had gone Pappy continued.

"According to Mira, she's the night manager for the restaurant and the bar, everything in those two places are on the up and up. The hostess's check ID's before anyone enters the bar and if the bar tenders or cocktail girls have any suspicions, they check them again. If a customer appears to have had too much, they cut em off."

"What about downstairs?" Matt asked. "Has he been able to get a look see about what goes on down there?"

"Mira does not get involved with what happens down there, but she knows what happens. There is another bar down there, they serve sandwiches and there are gambling tables, Blackjack, Poker and Craps. Here's the kicker. They operate as a private club. Only those who are members can even be in the place. Members can only enter through the door at the back of the building. Each member has a card that lets him into the building. Once inside, there's an attendant at the cloak room, who checks a roster and the members ID, and she then electronically opens the door leading into the club. The club operates Monday through Saturday from four pm and ceases business at two am just like any other business that sells alcohol."

"We probably need to check the law about gambling in the state," Matt stated. Pappy reached into the breast pocket of his shirt and took out a piece of paper that looked like it had come from a small notebook.

"Jim already has," Pappy said as he unfolded the paper and read from it. "Except as specifically authorized by statute, all forms of public gambling, lotteries, and gift enterprises are prohibited." Pappy folded the paper and looked over at Matt. "This indicates that only public games are illegal and that private games are not. They could very well be operating within the law."

"What about ladies of the night?" Matt was still curious. The waitress arrived with their order.

"Mira says that a member can bring in one female guest," Pappy related. "Other than that, there are females hired as cocktail hostesses. They are scantily clad and ensure that members are kept supplied with drinks and food and kept happy. There are three dressing rooms available for the ladies, there is a bed, and some stay over until daybreak after their shifts. It appears that any running of such illicit activity is unlikely."

"Sheriff Spence is going to be happy about this. We were both concerned that we would have a continuation of prior problems. If we don't get any complaints or things don't go sower in the future, we've got nothing to worry about."

Generally, on weekends Craig and Martha spent their time lounging together, often each reading a favorite book and snacking on delicacies that Kati had prepared and left for them. Katie until recently had volunteered at the Rock Springs Recreation Center, as a chaperone. This weekend however, they had traveled to Thermopolis, Wyoming and are visiting Canyon Acres, a retirement community situated along the Big Horn River amide the Hot Sulphur Springs.

Canyon Acres consisted of a rambling two story building complex that according to brochures encompassed five acres. The rest of twenty acres was dotted with cottages and duplex type structures. Most of the area surrounding the main building and the cottages was zero landscaped with desert plants and shrubs adorning the yards and entrances.

The three of them, Craig, Katie and Martha, walked up an inlayed brick walkway that passed through an attractive overhang to the automatic doors of the center's main entrance. They stepped into a well decorated atrium and as they stood admiring the lay out, to their left they could see a room where people were seated around tables playing what appeared to be card games; others were engaged in other games and there was a lot of shouting and cheering going on. To their right was the dining room. The tables were neatly set for the next meal with white napkins and real glasses, shining silver ware and white coffee cups, and there were people dressed in aprons and white caps scurrying around the room. They were greeted by a male person who had come from a small office in front of them.

"Welcome to Canyon Acres," the young man said. "My name is Craig; how may I be of assistance to you?"

"We've got something in common," Craig spoke up. "My name is Craig too, Craig Spence and this is my wife Martha and my daughter Katie." After the introductions and hand shaking Katie advised Craig, the facilities representative, that they were from Green River Wyoming and she had called a few days ago and made an appointment to visit."

"Oh yes!" the young man exclaimed. I'm the one who took your call. I'm the resident sales manager here. Please accompany me to the office and we'll start from there."

Craig, the facility sales manager went through his pitch, provided Craig and Martha brochures and explained floorplans for apartments and cottages, after which he escorted them through the main building pointing out the amenities and services that were available. Then he loaded them into a large golf cart and drove them through the cottages, stopping several times to allow them to see the different layout of floor plans. Lastly, he drove them along the river and showed them a small pier that extended from the property out into the river. There were several people fishing from the pier and others just sitting on benches, enjoying the view. Their escort seemed to be especially proud of the pier location and spoke highly of how the residents made use of it.

On the way back home, there was much conversation between Martha and Katie about what they had seen and the services that were offered at Canyon Acres. Finally, Martha turned to Craig, who was riding in the back seat and asked his opinion.

"Well dear, what did you think of the place," she asked. "Nice," Craig commented.

"Do you think you could live in a place like that?" There was a little sternness in her voice.

"You know," Craig began. "As we were going through, looking at the apartments and such, I was reminded of a story I read when I was a kid. It was about elephants. It was about this special place that they went when it was time to die. That's what I was reminded of. But I must say, life wouldn't be too shabby in a place like that. Little expensive though."

"That's just the first one we've looked at Dad." Katie spoke up as she maneuvered the car around the curves in the two-lane road leading out of town. "We'll look at some others in the next two or three weeks and see what they have to offer and compare prices."

"Elephants!" Martha was almost shouting. "Elephants? A special place to die. You have some special place in mind, other than a place like Canyon Acres, you'd like to die my husband?"

"No," Craig lamented as he watched the tumble weed covered fences go by. "I guess any old place will do."

There was little talk about the trip the rest of the way home or for the rest of the following week for that matter. No one, Craig, Martha or Katie mentioned anything. The time arrived for Katie to move and still no one brought up the matter. It was something that prayed on Craig's mind, however. He'd lived around the Rock Springs- Green River area most of his life and the idea of leaving the area didn't set well. He didn't know anybody in Thermopolis and what would he do with himself. As the days went by the idea of traveling and taking cruises did begin to appeal to him a little.

The commissioners hearing room was filled to standing room only the night they were supposed to have the first reading and vote on the proposal that Craig was interested in. After much discussion during other meetings the commissioners had dubbed the proposal "The Sweetwater

County Detention Center Project." It would be a long agenda because there was a period that citizens would have fifteen minutes to lodge complaints or make the commissioners aware of situations or conditions that they should take action on and there were other major projects to be discussed like low Income housing; allocation of funds for the county food bank; the Road and Bridge Department was presenting their annual proposed projects and funding request; The hospital was submitting its annual funding request also, and the community college was seeking support for a new wing. The sheet handed to Craig at the door showed that the reading of the detention proposal next to last. Unfortunately Craig had to sit up in the front row with the other department heads in case he had to respond to some situation or provide advice to the commissioners or a citizen, so he couldn't sneak out and mingle with people he knew that were gathered outside the chambers waiting for actions on whatever they were interested in.

Reluctantly Craig sat through an hour of public comment and then another hour and a half as the official agenda items were attended to which included long discussions by developers regarding land disputes in areas that they wanted to build multi-occupancy housing projects but were encountering fierce opposition from neighborhood citizen groups. When the detention center portion of the agenda was finally reached, Craig was surprised that there was a church group, represented by the churches minister, that spoke in opposition to the project. Unlike groups that were opposed to the developers, this group felt that the money should be used to build affordable housing for families rather than building a bigger jail that would serve to separate families. Craig was called upon to defend the detention center project. As he approached the podium, he tipped his hat, respectfully, to the minister prior to removing it and placing it on the podium in front of him and he began to speak.

"Mr. Chairman, Commissioner Delgado, Commissioner Cramer, Commissioner Sosa, Commissioner Kalinowski, for the record my name is Craig Spence and I'm the sheriff of Sweetwater County. Every year, for the past ten that I'm aware of, the commissioners have been petitioned to provide funding to bring the current county jail up to national standard and remodel to meet the increased requirements brought about by the tremendous increase in the county's population brought about by the production of oil and gas. Because of insufficient revenues, the county jail was always considered low priority and was left to languish, resulting in its deteriation and inability to adequately meet the county's needs." Craig paused for a second to let what he'd said soak in, then he continued.

"Conditions at the jail has led to several serious incidents, one which lead to the murders of three people and serious injury to others. The ACLU, after some negotiations with the county's governing body, filed suit to get conditions at the jail improved or get the jail closed. That lawsuit is still pending, but in the meantime, I'm restricted in the number of people that I can house in the jail and any overages I must transport to facilities in other counties that have been brought into compliance with state and national requirements. The cost to the county is overwhelming, and the sheriffs budget is having to be granted supplemental funding." Again, Craig let his statement sink in.

"The county was the recipient of nearly twenty million dollars last year from gas and oil revenue. It is recommended that these monies be used to construct a facility that will meet state and federal guidelines, that will comply with the terms of the ACLU's lawsuit and will adequately meet the county's needs."

After Craig finished, he took his hat put it on his head, again tipped it in the direction of the minister and took his seat. The county engineer was next, and he presented a preliminary drawing of what the detention center complex would look like and provided an estimated cost.

The project passed its first reading.

CHAPTER 8

THE DIVORCE BETWEEN Maggie and Ernest was not moving along as smoothly as Maggie would have liked. Even though lawyers were handling all the legal stuff, Ernest was not accepting the finality of the separation. She had moved out of the apartment that they had shared together in Rock Springs and had moved into an apartment in Green River. On one occasion she had noticed his truck, a large, black Dodge, with large wheels and a row of lights across the top of the cab, following at a distance when she turned into the parking lot at the complex where she had taken up residence. She hadn't mentioned it to Kevin, but she had seen the truck parked in the back of the parking lot when he picked her up in his Tan Ford Bronco.

Maggie and Kevin had gone on several dinner dates in recent weeks and she enjoyed being able to share her feelings and concerns with him. She told him that she was separated from her husband and why. She also told him how close she had come to having to prostitute herself and what she had to do to save herself. She was sure that Kevin would lose any interests that he may have had in her after he heard her confession, but when that didn't happen, she told him about Ernest following her and that she had seen his truck when they had gone to dinner together.

"You've filed for divorce and he's aware that you've filed, is that the case?" Kevin had inquired of her on one of their dinner dates.

"That's true." she had responded.

"Has he made any effort to make contact with you?" Kevin was a little concerned for her safety.

"No," Maggie responded, but he's always there."

"Have you given him any reason to believe that a reconciliation is possible?" Kevin wanted to make sure that he understood exactly what he might be getting into. He had become rather fond of Maggie.

"I was very emphatic when I left that it was over, and he had no reason to believe otherwise. Why are you interrogating me Kevin?" She sounded perturbed.

"I've gotten to like you a little Maggie," Kevin said rather sternly." I don't want anything to happen to you. You also have to remember that I'm an investigator and I want to know what the facts are."

They spent several moments emerged in their own thoughts and shoving the contents of their plates around. Each no longer interested in food. Kevin was the first to break the silence.

"I'm guessing," he began. "Because he hasn't tried to contact you, that he's hoping to force you to contact him. You know, he knows that you know that he's following you. He's trying to push you into making the first attempt at discussing the matter. I would suggest that you not do it. As long as he's just following you around and not causing any trouble, just let it ride. Be cautious though. When he doesn't get the reaction he wants, he'll probably change his tactics. How long do you think before things will be settled? The divorce I mean."

"There is a meeting scheduled with the attorneys next week," Maggie replied. "I think that is supposed to be the final meeting to determine how things will be divided up. I've already told my lawyer that I want nothing from him. I've got my job and want to just start over while I can. I think maybe I should move to a different apartment someplace else."

"And then what?" Kevin was a little gruff. "He'll follow you and find where you moved to. What do you do then, move again? When you see your lawyer at this meeting next week, you bring up the fact that he's been following you, right in front of him and his Lawyer. I'll bet there will be some fireworks."

Amy got to the hospital shortly after the ambulance had delivered Karen Moss. Karen was still on the gurney and was holding a blanket over her face and Amy could hear her sobbing. She didn't try to speak to Karen, and she didn't try to move the blanket. She just placed her hand on Karen's shoulder and left it there. Gradually the sobbing subsided, and Karen lowered the blanket and looked at this person who was trying to console her.

"Hi," Amy said softly with a smile on her face. "We're going to work our way through this but first we have to make sure that your needs are taken care of. When the Doctor finishes assessing your needs I'll take over and let you know how we'll go about things, Okay?

Karen nodded her head, indicating that she understood. She did not speak and when the Doctor came by to see her, she only answered questions that required a yes or no until she was asked about her medication regiment. She then related that she had been receiving Interferon once each week. When she was asked about the dosage, she stated that she was receiving thirty micrograms. When she was asked when she had received her last injection she couldn't remember.

When the Doctor finished, Amy along with one of the hospital's security people, pushed Karen to the lockup room. On the way Amy explained to her what she could expect so that she wouldn't be too shocked when she saw the bare room with only a bed. Karen did not react in any noticeable way to what she saw. She was still in her street clothes so when directed she took them off and donned a hospital gown that was on the bed. It was a slow process as she had difficulty coordinating her arm movements.

Once Amy had gotten Karen settled in, she called Joyce to replace her. Joyce is the security officer who had sat with Sister Patricia Anne while she was in detention. Joyce accompanied the charge nurse, Cookie Barns, into the room to conduct the check- in interview.

"Hello Karen," Cookie began. "I'm going to be asking you some questions so that we can get to know you better. Okay?"

"Okay," was the faint response from Karen.

"We know that your name is Karen Moss, and we know that you are married to Craven Moss. How old are you Karen?"

"I'm twenty-two," She replied. "My birthday is on 1 March 1960," "When were you first diagnosed with MS, "Cookie inquired. "When I was eighteen," Karen responded.

"How long have you been on the Interferon, "Cookie asked. "I don't know. A long time. Maybe two years."

"That's expensive stuff," Cookie commented. "Not that it's any of my business, but how did you pay for it?"

"My husband, Craven, had a great job as a long-haul truck driver. The insurance benefits were great. I used to go with him on the road. We'd sometimes be on the road for weeks at a time. When I got so I couldn't go with him anymore, and he had to spend time at home with me, they laid him off. Then his benefits ran out last month and here we are." Karen began to cry again.

"The side effects from interferon can be pretty awful," Cookie related. "Were you able to cope with them okay?"

"The effects from the Interferon was worse than the disease," Karen said. "I was sick all the time. There were times when I wished I was dead. I got an injection once every week. Just about time I'd begin to feel better after the last one I'd get another, and the terrible aftereffects would start all over."

"How long has it been since your last injection," Cookie asked. "Three weeks I think," Karen responded.

"OK, that's enough for now," Cookie said. "Let me take your temperature and blood pressure and we'll be all done."

"I've known several people who were diagnosed with MS," Joyce said to Cookie. "All of them eventually ended up in wheelchairs unable to move and slobbering over themselves. How does these interferons work?

"There are several different kinds of MS," Cookie began. Some are debilitating like you describe, others you wouldn't know the person had the disease unless they told you. Interferons are lab-made versions of the body's infection fighting protein. Doctors aren't sure but they think interferon turns down signals in the body that trigger the autoimmune response that leads to MS. They never went into it too thoroughly in nursing school, so I'm not really well versed on it."

Craven was brought up on charges of attempted robbery using a firearm, illegal possession of a firearm, and two counts of false imprisonment. Because all counts were Felonies his case would be prosecuted by the county attorney instead of the city attorney of Rock Springs. Craig paid Chief Matt Kessler a visit. After being seated Craig called Matt's attention to the Moss case.

"Matt," he began. "A public defender had that Moss kid to plead not guilty to four criminal counts brought by the City. You and I know that he's guilty, his attorney knows he's guilty and I can assure you that the county attorney knows that he's guilty and she's going to nail him to the wall. If he's convicted, that kid is going away for an awful long time."

"So far I agree with everything you said," Matt commented. After a brief pause Craig continued.

"In an act of desperation, he put several lives, including his own, in jeopardy. Fortunately, no one was hurt, and no loss was experienced." "What are you getting at Sheriff?" Matt was sure he wasn't going to like what was coming.

"This kid will have a big hunk of his life changed," Craig went on. "he'll survive it. I'm not sure his wife will. In any case, he's going to end up in the pen. It's going to cost the state a peck of money to keep him there. His wife is going to become a ward of the state, because she's got MS, no family to take care of her and she'll eventually be institutionalized."

"OK Craig." Matt said. "What cha got in mind?"

"What if," Craig started. "What if you and I could convince the city attorney, to write a letter to the county attorney, suggesting an alternative to jail time? Remember, this kid is a professional truck driver. Were he to be given a few years' probation and some form of community service, In this town or in this state, he'll have no problem getting a driving job; he'll be able to support himself; and he'll make enough money to get that medication for his wife that got him in this mess in the first place. I've already checked with the doughnut shop owner, and he has no wish to see this kid go to jail." Matt sat for a long moment, without blinking. Finally, he spoke.

"You know something Craig," Matt began. "When I grow up, I want to be just like you."

Craig had a suspicion that the efforts of his co-hart in law and he might have been successful when there was a message on his desk to call Sarah, the County Attorney. Before he made the call, he called Matt to see if he had gotten a copy of a letter written by the City Attorney. He had, Matt told him, but to his knowledge there had been no answer.

"I've got a message to call the County Attorney," Craig said. "I'll bet I'm about to get an answer." When he hung up Craig dialed Sarah's number.

"This is Sarah," she answered. "This is Craig, you called?"

"Weren't you expecting a call from me," Sarah asked with sarcasm. "Not quite so soon," Craig responded in kind.

"I just got a letter from the Rock Springs City Attorney," Sarah said. "It's written on his letter head, it's even signed by him, but it's got Craig Spence written all over it."

"Ya don't say," Craig quipped.

"Talk to me," she insisted. "The letter simply suggested that certain prosecutorial discretions be considered regarding the Moss case. What's the back story?"

Craig put both feet up on his desk, leaned way back in his chair and went through the events of the case, start to finish. Then he put his tag on it.

"I realize that it's not often that we get a case wrapped and sealed like this, but I also know that you aren't the type of prosecutor that's looking for fame and glory. Even though we both know that this kid is by no means innocent, there are extenuating circumstances that should encourage us to take another look. If we send this lad to the pen, we will have done him and his sick wife a terrible injustice. We can give them both a chance."

"What do you know about the wife's circumstances?" Sarah wanted to know.

"According to the reports that I've gotten from CPI, who's been guarding her," Craig related. "The hospital staff has arranged for her to join a study that's being conducted by an Oncologist up in Casper." There was a long pause. So long that Craig thought he might have been disconnected. "You there Sarah?"

"Yeh," she said. "I was just thinking, whenever you've brought me a case that you've been directly involved in, it's been a prosecutors dream. Always tied up nice and maybe not so neat but tied up. This is one of the few I can remember you being involved in, where no body died. I'll get with the court and see what we can work out."

"Thanks doll," Craig said.

It wasn't very often that Kevin was able to get away for a weekend. Even though he was not at the office, the lack of adequate manpower always required that he be readily accessible. This particular weekend Steve had agreed to hang around town so that Kevin could get away. He and Maggie had decided to just go for a nice long ride and maybe stop someplace and have lunch and then drive back to Green River. They decided to take highway 191 south out of Green River, to the south end of the Flaming Gorge Reservoir, and have lunch in the town of Dutch John which was a few miles into Utah and drive back.

They had just passed the road to Browns Park when Kevin noticed a large black pickup truck gaining on his Bronco from behind. As it got closer, he noticed that it was jacked up high and there was a light bar across the top of the cab. It was Ernest and as the truck approached it wasn't slowing down.

"Maggie," he said. "Brace yourself. I think we're in for a rough ride." Maggie turned and saw the truck now only a few feet from the back of the Bronco. The truck was so close that she couldn't see the front bumper.

"What's he doing," Maggie shouted.

"I think he's changing his tactics," Kevin said as he shoved the accelerator to the floor. The Bronco responded immediately and created some space between the two vehicles. The larger truck quickly closed the gap again and this time it bumped the back of the Bronco. Kevin managed to keep control and began to employ evasive maneuvers. As the big truck closed on him again Kevin moved to the north bound lane and quickly returned to the south bound lane. Luckily there was no north bound traffic. Kevin always had a department radio in his vehicle, and he reached for it.

"Dispatch-SO3," he said. "SO3-Dispatch," was the reply.

"SO3 traveling south on 191, approaching Utah border. Truck, Ford, Black in color, jacked up with large oversized tires, believed being driven by Ernest Gaither, attempting to run me off the road. Request assistance from Utah Patrol." Contact was again made to the back of the Bronco and Kevin dropped the radio in order to maintain control.

"SO3 you're fading out, say again your location." Maggie reached down near Kevin's feet. picked up the radio and squeezed the transmit button.

"South on highway 191 just crossing the Utah border." She yelled. The Bronco swerved violently and began to slide toward the right shoulder of the road. Kevin was trying desperately to keep the Bronco from going over the side into the bar ditch. The Bronco spun out and came to rest in the ditch on its side; on Kevin's side. Maggie had been thrown on top of Kevin who was yelling.

"My arm!! My arm is pined," he was yelling. The door had sprung open and his arm had gotten caught between the vehicle and the ground. Maggie, somewhat dazed was trying to dislodge herself from between the dashboard and the steering wheel. The radio was intermittingly transmitting.

"SO3 – Utah patrol--- your status----SO3 do---read." Kevin managed to find the radio that was lodged between him and the seat. As he was trying to adjust his body to get it out, the passenger door opened. Ernest reached down and grabbed Maggie's arm and pulled her kicking and screaming up through the door. Kevin finally got the radio and managed to key the transmit button with his free hand.

"SO3 off road in a ditch. I'm pined in. He's got Maggie!!

The suspension on the truck was not designed for high speeds on dirt roads. Ernest had left the main road and had taken a small dirt road that meandered through flat sagebrush covered terrain. The road was like a wash board and there were places where water had pooled during the winter snow runoff that made it very difficult to steer with one hand. He was using the other to block blows from Maggie who was flailing her arms and fists at his head.

"You're crazy," she shouted. "You've completely lost your mind. Let me out of this truck," she screamed. Finally, she realized that her pleas were in vain, and she stopped beating him. Her arms hurt anyway, and one side of her head was really sore. She put her hand there and felt a knot. She must have hit her head on something when the Bronco turned over.

"Where are we going," she asked in as calm a voice as she could. "I don't know," Ernest answered, and the sound of his voice had an I don't care quality to it. Maggie got a cold shiver. She began to realize that this ride might be her last. Calmly she tried to engage him. "Tell me what's going on Ernest," she asked. "And please, slow down. You're going to kill us both." God, she thought, I didn't mean to say that. Ernest did slow down a bit, but it was still a rough ride.

The Sheriff's office was in a panic. There was only a skeleton crew on, and the shift commander was out of his vehicle trying to shoo horses off the highway west of Green River. Apparently, he had left his handheld radio in the car because the dispatcher had been unable to raise him. Efforts to make contact with Sheriff Spence wasn't successful either. The dispatcher decided to contact the only deputy that was in the Green River and Rock Springs area today.

"SO10, Dispatch, respond please." Everything was quiet for a few moments, then the sound of a transmitter being keyed.

"SO10, go ahead."

"SO10," the dispatcher said breathlessly. "Kevin is in trouble. His radio was breaking up, but I believe he said that he was on Highway 191 and that he was being run off the road by Ernest Gaither."

"SO10, dispatch, where did he say he was on 191?"

"A female came on and said the Utah Border," the dispatcher said. "I've already contacted the Utah Highway Patrol --Stand by phone ringing," the dispatcher said. There was a long period of silence before the dispatcher came back on.

"SO10, the dispatcher at Dutch John Utah reports that a patrol unit has located Kevin's Bronco," the dispatcher related. "He's waiting to get a status report." Again, there was a long silence. Finally, SO10 broke in.

"Dispatch, I know where Sheriff Spence is," he said. "I just left him and his wife at the Chinese restaurant in Rock Springs. I'll go back and see what he wants us to do."

"10-4 S010," the dispatcher responded. "I'll contact you as soon as I hear from Dutch John."

Because of the increased competition, Fred and Amy had sought to diversify their services so as to remain competitive. After researching costs experienced by enforcement agencies in all twenty- three counties in Wyoming, they found that one of the greatest impacts was the movement of persons from one jurisdiction to the other.

The tremendous influx of persons to the state as a result of the oil and gas boom, put a strain on the resources of the already underfunded and undermanned county enforcement agencies. Persons arrested in one county for infractions were often found to be wanted in other counties and sometimes in other states. In those circumstances either the arresting agency had to deliver that person to the county in which the warrant was issued, or the issuing county had to retrieve persons being held by another county. This increased transportation costs and manpower shortages not to mention personnel overtime costs.

Fred had a commercial pilots license. He and Amy determined that if they were to provide an air service to agencies throughout the state, counties would be able to realize a considerable savings, monetarily and manpower wise. They promoted the idea to county representatives in the twenty-three counties and surprisingly got a positive reception from the most heavily populated counties. They agreed to a one-year trial and CPI purchased a Cessna 206, that could carry six people including the pilot and scheduled flights twice a week to pick up and deliver wanted persons to the appropriate jurisdictions. Sweetwater County Commissioners agreed to add the service to CPI's existing contract.

As soon as Craig was advised of Kevin's situation and the apparent kidnapping of Maggie, he immediately instructed the department's dispatcher to contact CPI and see if the plane was available. It was, and Craig arranged to meet Fred at the airport where he would brief him.

Almost as soon as the two were airborne, they could see highway 191 so Fred maneuvered the plane in a southerly direction toward the town of Dutch John, Utah. As they approached the town Craig contacted Kevin on his radio.

SO3, this is SO1, do you read?"

SO1 I read you loud and clear," was the reply from Kevin. SO3, what is your status," Craig asked.

SO1 my vehicle has been placed back of the road by Dutch John towing and I'm mobile again," Kevin said.

SO3, I'm airborne with CPI 1," Craig advised. "We are approaching Dutch John at this time. Do you have any idea which way that truck went?"

SO1, I was pinned down," Kevin stated, "I didn't see which way it went but by the sound of it I think it took the road toward Flaming Gorge reservoir."

Having monitored the conversation between the two lawmen, Fred banked the plane to the right and took up a course over the reservoir that positioned Craig so he could see all of the roads and trails that Ernest might have taken.

Kevin in the meantime had taken a Browning 22 semi-auto rifle that he used to shoot prairie dogs, from a rack in the back of his Bronco, put it between the two front seats and was proceeding along the main dirt road on the east side of the lake. He could see CPI 1's plane ahead in the distance.

Ernest had turned off the main dirt road along the east side of the lake and had taken a trail that went over a ridge and down into a draw. An old abandoned ranch house sat in a grove of trees and Ernest pulled the truck under the trees in back of the house and turned off the engine.

"Maggie, I don't want us to be divorced," he said.

"Don't you understand Ernest, "She said. "It's done, over, the relationship has been destroyed, there is nothing left to save."

"I know everything is my fault Maggie, but I can change," Ernest pleaded.

"If you could have, you would have Ernest," Maggie responded. "I'm going on with my life and you need to go on with yours, without me.

Ernest began to sob; tears ran down his face into his mouth and his body shook for a moment. Then he became calm, very quiet. He reached down in front of the driver's seat and pulled out a handgun.

Fred had reached the northern most part of the lake, made a wide right-hand turn and headed south along the eastern side of the highway when Craig reached over and touched his arm. Over the planes intercom Craig almost shouted.

"I saw the reflection of the sun off of something down there in the trees by that ranch house." Fred banked the plane so he too could see. Sure enough, there was a truck down there. Fred turned the plane away from the site as if leaving the area. He climbed to a higher altitude and flew back over the lake.

SO3, this SO1. We've spotted him. He's in a draw behind an old ranch house," Craig advised. "I also see your vehicle. In about a quarter of a mile turn right and go up over the hill. When you get to the top of the hill you should be able to see the ranch house. He's in the back under some trees."

"10-4 SO1," Kevin responded and followed Craig's directions. Sure enough, when he topped the hill, he could see the house but could not see the truck. It wasn't far across the draw to the house, so he parked the Bronco and with his rifle, took off on foot, using growths of pinion trees as cover.

"If you're trying to scare me, you've done it," Maggie said. Her voice was trembling. She managed to get it under control. "Have you lost your mind. What are you planning to do?"

"If you're gone, I don't think I want to live anymore," Ernest said in almost a whisper. "I don't want to lose you Maggie." Ernest was holding the revolver in his lap. Maggie couldn't help staring at it. While doing so she noticed the door lock indicator on the driver's side door. He hadn't locked the doors. She sat up with her back against the door on her side. She kept talking as she slipped her left hand behind her back, fishing for the latch.

"Don't you understand Ernest. You've already lost me. Killing yourself- or me won't change that. You need to pull yourself together and go on with your life." She found the latch, pulled it, shoved the door open and fell out on the ground. She got to her feet and ran, darting around and behind pinion trees. She heard the pop of the revolver, and she ran. There was another pop and she heard the bullet tear through a tree to her right, and she ran. She came to a small arroyo and tumbled down its bank to its sandy bottom. She landed on her hands and knees. She was exhausted, she couldn't run any more. She heard yelling, but her heart was beating so loud in her ears she couldn't understand.

"Hey – Ernest- over here," Kevin was yelling. Ernest was distracted. He was now trying to see where this voice was coming from. Kevin had taken cover behind a well-developed pinion. He could see Ernest, but Ernest could see him. His rifle was resting on the base of a branch and he could scc Ernest through the varmint scope mounted on top.

"Drop the weapon Ernest," Kevin called out. Ernest pointed the revolver in the direction that Kevin's voice was coming from and Kevin fired. The bullet struck Ernest just above the left knee and he yelped and crumbled to the ground.

"Are you going to drop that gun or am I going to have to pick you apart a little at a time," Kevin shouted. Ernest threw the revolver a few feet away from him. The pain in his leg was excruciating. Cautiously Kevin approached him, picked up the revolver and ejected the rounds from the cylinder.

Kevin took a set of cuffs, that he always carried stuck in his belt at the small of his back, And secured Ernest's arms behind his back. He then took his radio from his hip pocket.

"SO1 this is 3," was his transmission. "3 this is SO1, go ahead," was the reply.

"This is 3, Subject in custody," Kevin advised.

"10-4 SO3, what's the status of the girl? Craig asked.

"Don't rightly know," Kevin said. "When I came up on the scene, this guy was shooting at her as she was running through the trees. Don't think she was hit. Can you circle the area and see if you can see her? Can't be far." There was a pause and Craig came back on.

"10-4 SO3, we're in route to your location."

Kevin could hear the airplanes engine, but Fred had kept the airplane on the other side of the hill so as not to alert Ernest that he was being watched from the air.

Maggie was sitting in the sandy arroyo, with her back against the bank. She wondered if Ernest was looking for her; should she get up and run or should she stay put; If he found her would he shoot her and leave her body in the arroyo; she didn't want to die she was thinking, Before she could decide what to do, an airplane had come from behind her, very low, and she watched as it turned and headed back toward the ranch house. She continued to sit, pondering what that was all about. She heard the airplane coming back and it again had come very close and turned back toward the house. This time she had seen someone waving and pointing toward the ranch house. She got up, climbed the bank and slowly walked through the trees toward where Ernest had parked the truck. The airplane was circling now, and she could see the truck. She also recognized Kevin standing over Ernest who was lying on the ground. She began to run. As she came into sight Kevin, looked up from tending Ernest's leg and called out to her.

"Hey! The way you were running I thought you'd be in Dutch John by now," he quipped.

Maggie was running and crying. All the tension and fear that had built up during the ordeal came pouring out as she threw her arms around Kevin and buried her face in his shoulder.

"I thought I was going to die," she said between sobs. Kevin again took to his radio.

"SO1 this SO3," he said.

"So1 here," Craig replied.

"SO1 this is 3, all's well," Kevin reported. "We do need an ambulance though."

"SO3, who's hurt," Craig asked.

"SO1 this is 3, I had to get the subjects attention and he sustained a bullet wound to the leg," Kevin replied.

"10-4 SO3," Craig acknowledged. "I'll have dispatch contact Dutch John and have them send the medics out. Fred is going to land on that straight stretch of road and let me off where you turned off. I'll ride the ambulance up, and you can ride to Green River with your prisoner and I'll bring Maggie and the Bronco. I'll also have Dutch John send a tow truck out to get the pickup."

"10-4 SO1 we'll be waiting for ya," Kevin said.

Everything worked as planned. Fred landed and took the plane off without incident; Craig rode the ambulance up to the old ranch house; the medics did what they had to do to the gunshot wound; Kevin rode in the ambulance to Green river and Craig followed with the Bronco.

At the jail Kevin booked Ernest in on two charges, Vehicular Assault for pushing the Bronco off the road and Attempted Murder for shooting at Maggie. Those charges made sure Ernest would not be able to bond out.

CHAPTER 9

I T WAS A long day for Craig, the Kevin and Ernest Gaither thing had worn him out. It was nice to finally be in the solitude of his home. He was somewhat surprised however; Martha didn't greet him, and he could hear no movement around the house. As he entered the kitchen there Martha was, standing at the stove, apparently stirring something in a saucepan.

"Hello Doll," he said rather sheepishly. Martha turned slightly to casually glance at him but said nothing. She returned her attention to stirring.

"Would it be better if I went out and came in again, "Craig inquired.

"No," Martha said emphatically.

"Want to tell me what you've got stuck in your craw?" Craig was curious.

"I called your office to see if you wanted anything special for dinner," Martha began. "At first I thought the girl who answered was being rude but then I realized she was talking on the radio and must have taken the phone receiver off its cradle and laid it down. Finally, she asked if I could call back and hung up. While she was talking, I got parts of her transmissions, something about dutchy ditch in Utah and you involved in chasing a kidnapper. What the heck were you doing in Utah? You are not a young man anymore and you need to stop acting like one."

Craig sat quietly for a moment, letting what Martha said sink in. "Dutchy Ditch" he was thinking. A snicker almost came out, but he knew better than to be cavalier about this. She is really upset, he was thinking. He pulled out a chair from the kitchen table and spoke softly and slowly.

"Martha," he said. "Come sit."

"I can't, need to stir this gravy," she replied.

"To hell with the gravy, come sit," Craig was not asking, and Martha knew it. She stopped stirring the saucepan and sat. Craig began to explain the situation.

"Kevin was in trouble and when I heard about It, I did what I had to do. He was run off the road and he ended up in a ditch near Dutch John Utah. He was traveling with Maggie Gaither. She is the Secretary at the rock Springs Police Department, and she is in the process of getting a divorce.

"Oh, Oh," Martha said with a sigh. "Is Kevin the cause?"

"No, they didn't start seeing each other until sometime after she had filled. Anyway, she rode back to Green river in the Bronco with me. She said that Ernest, her husband, thought in his misguided way that he'd try and convince her not to go through with the divorce. So, he ran Kevin off the road and dragged Maggie out of the Bronco and drove off with her. I got Fred over at CPI to take me up in his airplane, we spotted Ernest's truck and Kevin was able to take him down. Only Ernest was hurt. Kevin put a bullet in his leg."

"I'm sure there's much more to the story," Martha said looking at him down her nose with some suspicion. "I suppose I should just be thankful that you're home safe and sound."

"Dutchy Ditch?" Craig said, wrinkling his nose and looking sidewise at her with questioning eyes. They looked at each other quietly for a second and then both burst into uncontrollable laughter. That is until they began to smell the gravy burning.

At the office the following morning, Craig had a few moments before the staff meeting so he took the time to glance at the days edition of the newspaper. It never ceased to amaze him how reporters managed to get information so wrong and how talented they were at sensationalizing it. It wasn't the headline of the day, but it was located prominently on the front page. *"Local man, Ernest Gaither, wounded in gun fight after confronting sheriff's officer on highway 191. The Sheriff's officer, Detective Kevin Marcy, was apparently on a weekend jaunt with Mr. Gaither's estranged wife, Maggie, who is and employee at the Rock Springs Police Department. Some type of altercation ensued after Mr. Gaither ran the officer off the road and removed Mrs. Gaither from Marcy's vehicle."*

The article went on for several paragraphs highlighting Kevin's years of service with the department and explaining how Ernest had been cornered near Dutch John, Utah and shots had been fired resulting in Ernest being wounded. Only in the very last few lines of the final paragraph did the article read: *"Mr. and Mrs. Gaither had been separated for a time and Mrs. Gaither had filed for divorce."*

When he entered the conference room everyone had already seated themselves around the table. Craig walked over to Kevin and handed him the paper over his shoulder.

"You made front page," Craig said as Kevin took the paper. The others, Sherrie and Steve, made teasing comments. "Ooo, we have a celebrity amongst us," Sherrie said and Steve Teased," You'll never live this down Ole Buddy."

"Reporters have been calling all morning," Sherrie informed. "Do you want the calls transferred to your office or what?" Kevin was busy reading the article and didn't answer right away and Sherrie prodded. "Hey Romeo, did you hear me?"

"Hey, come on you guys," Kevin said as he put the paper down, a little embarrassed. "There's nothing juicy here, we were just going for a ride. As for the reporters, they can get copies of the report I submitted regarding the incident and that's all they'll get."

"Nice plan," Craig commented. "I see that you don't know these newspaper guys when they think there's a story hidden in this. If they can't get you on the phone, they'll show up wherever you go. I'd suggest that you talk to them and get it over with. Tell them that you and Maggie are friends. It was a beautiful day and you decided to go for a ride. No matter how many of them try and make something other than that out of it, stick to your story. You'd better get with Maggie and make sure she feels the same way you do. Not exactly the right time for a surprise." Kevin looked up and their eyes met. There was a gleam of sorts in Craig's and Kevin understood what he was trying to tell him.

"May I be excused for a minute Sheriff?" Kevin asked and Craig nodded his head in the affirmative.

"Sherrie," Craig began. "What's going on?"

"you recall the teen that was in detention and we arrested her father for molesting her? Well, she's back. The court released her to her mother and things seemed to be okay at home, but things weren't good at school. Word got around about what had happened to her. I guess from what I understand, the girls shunned her mostly, but they were always snickering when she'd walk by and the boys kept yelling at her and saying how much better it would be with them instead of her old man. She broke and tried killing herself again. This time she slit her wrist."

"Kids can be brutal," Craig said with sorrow in his voice. "That girl is gonna have to dig deep to find self-worth, and she's gonna need a lot of help. What' the plan, do you know?"

"According to CPI, she is going to be provided counseling while she's in detention and the mother has family back east and as soon as she is released this time they're leaving."

"Anything else going on," Craig asked.

"I put a note on your desk yesterday from the county commissioner's office. They want you to give them a call. The jail population is down to twenty inmates. So, we're well in compliance with the court's ruling.

We have sixteen that are being held by other counties. That's about it. Things are slow."

"Slow is good," Craig replied. "Steve, what's keeping you busy." "I'm in the process of conducting the annual inventory of the department Sheriff, "Steve said. "I'm having the section chiefs send me their actual count and I'll compare them to the master inventory

list. If there are differences, then I plan to have those section chiefs explain why those differences exist. Sometimes it's because items have been moved to another section or they may have been sent to salvage or whatever. We will have to explain to county property managers why any items may be missing."

"How do things look so far?" Craig asked.

"I've only gotten a couple of reports from the section chiefs so far and they look pretty good. The larger sections haven't responded yet," Steve replied. Just as he completed his response to Craig, Kevin returned to the table. Craig couldn't tell from his facial expression weather he had gotten good news or if things were unraveling So, he asked.

"Well, how did things go?"

"Maggie has already been contacted by the media," Kevin began. "She referred all their questions about the case to this office. As for the questions about any relationship with me she says that she explained that because of the coordination that occurs between the City PD and the SO, that she has known me for some time and that recently we had worked a project together and I became aware of her stressing over her pending divorce. She shared with them that I had offered to take her for a ride, just to get away, and she accepted. She says she also told them that there's nothing there, just an innocent ride that didn't work out too well."

"Sounds to have some finality to it, but one never knows when it comes to an aggressive reporter," Craig contributed. "Anything else occupying your time?"

"Not really sir, but the county attorney says that I need to attach statements from you and Fred to my report. She'd like to have those as soon as possible so she can file the charges," Kevin replied.

"You bet," Craig said. I'll get with Fred and we'll get those to you today. I'll be in the office all day if you need me, in the meantime, carry on."

Back in his office, Craig found two pieces of paper on his desk. One was the message that Sherrie had put there telling him to call Raul and the other was a note from the commissioner of elections office. It said, "DEADLINE TO FILE YOUR INTENTION TO RUN ONLY 4 DAYS AWAY."

Craig sat back in his office chair; his body actually gone limp. He had no idea that time had crept up on him like this. As he sat there unbelieving, his eyes wandered around the office and fell upon the mementoes that had been collected over the years; the glass cases in which weapons that had been confiscated from not so nice people were displayed; other display cases that multiple types of drug paraphernalia was show cased. The pictures on the wall of fellow lawmen who had lost their lives in the line of duty. Another picture, one of Martha, that he kept on his desk caught his eye and he leaned forward, took it in his hands and stared at it for a long minute.

After replacing Martha's picture back where it had smiled at him for so many years, he opened the upper right-hand desk drawer and took out the holstered thirty-eight special. If it could talk, would have some interesting stories to tell. He replaced the weapon and closed the desk drawer.

He reached over and pulled his phone closer to him. After taking the receiver from its cradle he pushed the button that connected him to the office of his administrative assistant.

"Good morning Sheriff," came a female voice. "I have nothing on your schedule today."

"That's scary," Craig joshed. "Would you please get the Election Commissioner's office on the line and patch him through to me?"

THE END

"Greyhound Therapy" _Undermanned and overwhelmed, the sheriff is faced with an exploding population, having to solve a murder that occurred in his jail, the sheriff must use all his ingenuity and problem solving ability as he deals with crime, personal struggles in his own life and carrying out his responsibilities. This thrilling and touching novel shows that tragedy and adversity can bring people together in a common purpose of caring for what is truly important in our lives.

"After the Ride" _Authorities and mental health institutions sometimes find it more economical or convenient to furnish individuals a bus ticket rather than, for what ever reason, meet their needs. Most transients that arrive in Rock Springs by bus, voluntarily or involuntarily; often in need of stabilizing medications, get to meet Sheriff Craig Spence. though undermanned and with few resources, strives to deal with the undesired transient influx and criminal activity resulting from their presence.

As sheriff of Sweetwater County, Craig Spence has established himself as the ultimate crime fighter. He also is reputed to be a shrewd politician, a skill that is most beneficial in public service. In Craig Spence's county, he often matches wits with activist organizations and county leaders. while he is often involved in the pursuit of criminals, enforcement of the law is most often not run of the mill.

JR Conway, born in Washington DC in 1931. Retired Military, retired Law Enforcement. 12 years Private Investigator and owner of 240 employee security company.

ISBN 979-8-89391-101-5

SOMEONE
ELSE'S
CASTLE
SHORT STORIES
J.H. TOMEN